WISE ENOUGH
TO BE **FOOLISH**

WISE ENOUGH
TO BE FOOLISH

A novel based on a true story

GAURI JAYARAM

Dearest Ashritha,

Wishing you the very best!

Love,

Gauri

JAICO PUBLISHING HOUSE

Ahmedabad Bangalore Bhopal Bhubaneswar Chennai
Delhi Hyderabad Kolkata Lucknow Mumbai

Published by Jaico Publishing House
A-2 Jash Chambers, 7-A Sir Phirozshah Mehta Road
Fort, Mumbai - 400 001
jaicopub@jaicobooks.com
www.jaicobooks.com

© Gauri Jayaram

WISE ENOUGH TO BE FOOLISH
ISBN 978-81-8495-456-2

First Jaico Impression: 2013

Page design and layouts: Special Effects, Mumbai

Printed by
Repro India Limited
Plot No. 50/2, T.T.C. MIDC Industrial Area
Mahape, Navi Mumbai - 400 710

A sister is the greatest gift of life.
Dedicated to my favourite girls
Mishtu, Geeta, Aprajita and Gayatri
The world is yours and may you live a beautiful life
— exactly as you please!

To protect the identity of the people in the story, almost everyone's name in the book has been changed. A few parts of the story have also been fictionalised for the same reason.

ACKNOWLEDGEMENTS

When you finish putting 28 years of your life in a book, there will be a lot of people to thank. To everyone who is in the book, my sincerest thanks, for without you there would be no tale to tell. The fact that you are part of this story goes to show your importance in my life.

For the sake of a tightly knit plot, some of you had to be merged into single characters. So this would be a good time to thank you for being a part of my life – after all you contributed to the plot – Ruchin, Piyush, Aruna, Rhitu and Rajashree.

Mouli, Deepa, Bilkish, Sanjoo, Devendra and Suhail: thank you for the time and effort spent on reading the first draft. Without your honest opinions and encouragement, this book would have stayed on my hard-drive forever. And Shashi and Raghu – thanks for not reading it!

I owe it to Nikhil and Aparna for telling me to write the book in the first place.

Divya Dubey – you are the best editor. Thank you for your earnestness and for always believing in my manuscript.

Thank you Jaico, for publishing the book and for being the very nice people that you are. Nalini and Anuja, thank you for helping me with the pre-launch work.

To Aprajita, my first born who gives me peace, and adorable little Gayatri, who knows that the F-word is not 'fish' – thank you for your love, for making me laugh and for putting up with my absence as I spend oodles of time pursuing things that make me 'me'. May you grow up to be bright, independent and happy young women, with the power to make India the country we want it to be!

And to my better half who completes me. Without you, our daughters would miss their school bus every day, my dream job would be my worst nightmare and I would have to change the ending of my story. You are my rock. Thank you for being you and for giving me a wonderful family!

I am grateful to God for the way he has planned my existence. The way he has allowed and continues to allow many people to touch my life on a regular basis, so I can do the things I am meant to do. Thank you Manjula, thanks to my colleagues at work and in the travel industry, to my running buddies, my classmates at IIM-B and to my extended family.

PROLOGUE

July 11, 1998. Saturday.
Netherlands is playing against Croatia to fight for third place in the FIFA World Cup.

Sitting alone on my double bed, I am trying to make sense of what is going on in my world. For a girl 'socially' married just four months ago, to be sitting by herself on a weekend, not aware of where her husband might be, is difficult to comprehend. But, this has been going on for sometime now.

The World Cup started a few weeks ago, and every time I ask my husband where he was the previous evening, I am told, 'Watching football'.

'With whom?'

'Friends.'

'What friends?'

'You don't know them.'

And so it goes on day after day.

Have you ever tried to count the number of tear-jerkers we watch in a lifetime? Those movies that make us cry in the theatre as we hope that no one has noticed us wiping our tears, and at times, blowing our nose too? We love them. They're just movies after all. Then we hear real stories about people losing those they love. These are other people's stories. These things don't happen to ordinary people — like me. And at twenty-six, I have no idea that I am part of a universe where everything evens out. Why should I have to deal with anything terrible in my life?

∼

Two weeks ago, I sat up till five in the morning wondering where he was, morbid thoughts took over my brain. Maybe he had been run over by a bus. Or murdered on some dingy street while returning from a pub? Maybe I should call the police? Thankfully, I called his friends first.

Now, how would you like to be woken up at five on a Saturday morning if you had just returned home from a party a couple of hours earlier?

But they were his friends. I thought they would understand. 'I am really sorry to call you at this hour but…is he with you? He hasn't been home all night. He said he was going to watch football with some friends.'

He wasn't with any of his friends I knew. But the keywords here are 'I knew', because he had suddenly added a whole lot of names to his list of friends I didn't know. After exhausting the numbers I did have, I evaluated my options.

I started calling my friends. 'Hi, it's me. I am sorry to call so early, but he hasn't been home the entire night. What should I do? Could you please drive me around so that we could look for him?'

Most of them tried to comfort me.

He will be home. I am sure nothing has happened to him. Give it some more time. Let's wait a bit. Call me if he's not back in a couple of hours.

They were right. He did get home, even if it was after sunrise. I couldn't decide whether I should be relieved that he was alive, or angry that I had been put through an entire night of stress and misery. Sometimes, when you realise that the demons are in your head, and that reality is not so bad, you cry out of relief. I started crying when I saw him. I asked him where he had been, and we had the same conversation all over again.

'I was watching football at a friend's.'

'Which friend?'

'You don't know him.'

'Why couldn't you call up to tell me where you were? And why didn't you come home all night?'

'He doesn't have a phone yet. We drank till late, so I decided to stay back. Everyone stayed back.'

How should I react? Should I scream at him? Should I ignore him and stop talking to him — as in, you know, *punish* him? That's what we girls do. Maybe I should stay calm and say, 'Hey, we need to talk.'

I wondered how difficult it was to find a phone. The late '90s was not the mobile phone era, but we were not exactly living in the dark ages.

'Do you know how worried I have been? I sat here all night… thinking of the worst things, wondering if you were dead or alive. I called every person we know, and I don't deserve to go through this!' I screamed.

'You are the one putting yourself through it. I don't control your feelings… *you* do. It's not my fault that you choose to entertain bad thoughts. Next time, I suggest you go to sleep, because you can see that I am fine and that it was not worth the effort. And please don't go around calling people at unearthly hours. I will leave you a note the next time I am out.' His voice was calm.

My brain tried to understand this new perspective. It was true that those dark thoughts were self-invented, but there was a good reason for it. Yes, I had some power over my feelings, but it was his behaviour driving them out of control. How did he manage it? I was the hurt party here. I was right, and he was wrong, but at this moment, it seemed just the opposite.

～

That was two weeks ago.

Today is July 11, and here I am again. Today, there is a post-it on the mirror: *Going to watch football. May not be back tonight.*

Okay, at least I won't be spending another night waiting and wondering. This is better… definitely. But I read the note again and think that '*may not* be back' means he definitely won't be back tonight. And now I want to know why.

I flip some channels. I try to be interested in who will win the World Cup. The finals will be played between Brazil and France tomorrow, but I don't seem to care though I am a football fan. Or maybe I am not. I try to find a movie to watch, but I am not really paying any attention. My mind seems to be having a conversation with itself.

'What sort of marriage is this?'

'A modern-day marriage. He does his own thing, and I do my own, and, as life goes on, we will find the time to do things together. Many people also call this "space".'

These days there seems to be more 'space' in my marriage than togetherness. I can count on my fingertips the hours we spend together in a day (without having to use both hands, or even all fingers on one hand). We spend most of our waking hours at work, and travelling to office, and back. It's the usual Bombay life — living in the suburbs and working in the city. Somewhere along the line, things changed. The distance between us is growing.

'How do millions of married couples manage to keep the spark alive?' I ask myself. It's unlikely that I am the only one suffering from the Big City Syndrome.

What annoys me most is how everything seems so cryptic when it comes to our relationship. No questions have any straight answers. He makes strange comments, and has strange views. I like my life in two colours — black and white, but it seems a murky grey at this point on this Saturday night. I don't like this feeling, and I really don't know how I am to deal with this situation, because the problem itself is unclear.

My mind strays to the previous evening. I was at a temple, Siddhi Vinayak, a famous landmark in Bombay. This was a rare visit for a person like me. I stopped going to temples many years ago. I had seen too many overweight priests trying to make a quick buck from those who desperately needed their prayers to be heard. Then, on one of my rare visits to make an attempt to re-establish my faith in 'places of worship', I developed an awful headache. Going to God's 'home' should have made it better. But the place was so crowded that I was pushed and pulled in different directions. And, as I begged God to help me get rid of my headache, someone set the bells ringing, and everyone began to screech (or was it sing?) in high-pitched voices. How could God ever hear me? I was convinced that he would never even notice I was there. I was much better off talking to him on my own private hotline.

And, in any case, the prayers were in Sanskrit. That was

the only subject I had consistently failed in, and I figured that if I didn't understand what I was saying, I could end up saying something exactly the opposite of what I meant. Though I had travelled the distance from being born with no faith — as most of us are before our brains are coloured with the beliefs of our near and dear ones — to somehow learning to trust God over the years, I just could not correlate my visits to the temple and their final outcome. Apart from that headache incident, that is.

But, on Friday morning, Gayatri called me to accompany her to Siddhi Vinayak. While it was not a perfect meeting place, I justified the temple visit as an excuse for a rendezvous with a good friend, and agreed. Yes, I know it's not exactly why people go to temples, but we hadn't met for many months. It was great to see her, and I didn't mind the noise or the crowd because she and I were busy catching up on old times and gossip. It took us more than an hour to get to Ganeshji's idol where people offered their prayers.

She gave me flowers from her basket, and told me to pray. I did as I was told. After all, I was born a Hindu Brahmin. And even if going to temples was a challenge, I did know how to pray. But today Gayatri was a little pushy. She told me to ask God to help me. I was not in a mood to get into a discussion about *why*. She didn't know anything about the situation at my home yet — mostly because there was nothing to say. I could not put my finger on what was wrong myself. We left the temple, and soon it was time to say goodbye. We hugged each other, and I stopped a cab. Just as I was slipping inside, she grabbed me and said, 'Listen, girl, you need to learn to rely on yourself. Don't trust everyone in life.'

I looked at her blankly. She knew I would want to know why she had said that. Before I could react, she pushed me into the cab, shut the door, and walked away in the opposite direction.

She was gone. And I only had myself to ask why she had said that. It was a sweeping statement — 'Don't trust everyone in life'. Is trust important? Maybe. Maybe it is trust and not love that is the foundation of every positive relationship. If a teacher didn't trust a student to realise his potential, the student would never have the confidence to attempt anything. If a child didn't trust her mother to protect her, she would never try to discover the world beyond her home. If a colleague didn't trust others to do the jobs they are assigned, no work would ever get done. And what if one spouse didn't trust the other? It would be an empty and meaningless relationship.

This was just yesterday. Today, once again, I am trying to make sense of what she said. Maybe she had some idea of what was going on in my life. It is a bit like when you steal a bite of something from the fridge, and think no one will know, because you can't see the crumbs on your own face.

The special thing about Gayatri is that she isn't just my friend, she is one of the few common friends my husband and I have. He thinks I have too many friends and that it makes my relationships meaningless. He says that quality and quantity cannot co-exist. Most of my other friends are too wild, obnoxious, loud, and even 'shallow' for him, but Gayatri is not. And, she is beautiful.

How can things change so suddenly and quickly? How can a person change so soon? There must be something. I can feel my grey cells rev up to understand what had happened to us, to me.

'Open his office bag,' my inner voice says clearly. The bag is on the table.

'It doesn't belong to me, it's his,' another voice replies. I have never touched his things.

But this voice is very strong, like God sitting in my head trying to help me.

'Shut up and open the bag.'

And so the voices, the grey cells, and my conscience succumb and the contents of my husband's bag are now on the bed. The same double bed that we have made love on innumerable times. I have been sitting alone on it for the last three hours. My hands tremble.

This is when it hits me. The grey in my life has suddenly changed into black and white.

There are no tears, but I cannot breathe. This cannot be happening. Slowly, the shock turns to rage, and my mind races to figure out what I should do. I was sure that if this ever happened to me, I would die. This is what happens in other people's lives. It happens in movies, and to the neighbour's neighbour — people who lead a different life. It doesn't happen to people like me, who have a predictable day-to-day existence. My life is at the crossroads and about to change forever.

Chapter 1

I am not sure why History was my least favourite subject in school. I hated it even more than I hated Physics. Funnily enough, as soon as I left school, I developed a love for the subject. I don't know how that happened either. They say that to know where you are going, you have to first know where you come from. So, I have to start from the very beginning — history.

The story actually started in 1972, just after the war between India and Pakistan. I know this makes an awfully unhappy beginning, but trust me, this part of the story was not in my control. As a pilot in the Indian Air Force, my father fought in that war, and his cousin, who was also in the Air Force, was declared 'missing-in-action' in the enemy territory. I was supposed to be born on December 25, but I decided to postpone my arrival since the situation was not very pleasant.

Thus, I missed sharing my birthday with the most famous man in history ever — Jesus Christ (though we do share our sun sign), and ended up with the same birthday as Sir Isaac Newton, Louis Braille, and other such mortals, i.e. January 4. You know that the date and time of your birth determine your destiny. Maybe the situation then — the animosity between India and Pakistan after Independence, the choice of my father's career, the subsequent wars, the disappearance of my father's cousin, and my delayed entry into the world — all this sealed my fate.

My parents gave me a name, but a few months later, my

father decided to change it. My new name was Gauri — another name for Goddess Parvati, the daughter of the mountains, the mother Goddess, and the wife of Shiva — the first lady of Hindu mythology, was what my mother always insisted.

My father was the happiest man in the world. He had longed for a princess in the family, and finally, I had arrived. He nursed dreams of how I would grow up to be his perfect little girl — delicate, pretty, well-mannered, with all the qualities of a future home-maker and how, in due course, he would find me a suitable groom. His friends and family would be proud of what he had produced, and he would give me away with sadness in his eyes as I wept at being separated from my home, and then I would live happily ever after. Alas, this was a dream that always remained a dream, for I turned out to be nothing like that.

My mother was all of twenty years old when I was born, so we were not an adult and a child, we were two children. She had been married to a man her parents had chosen for her, and like most women of her generation and she had never had a boyfriend. She had dropped out of college because her father had found her a 'suitable match' — a well settled Punjabi boy from the armed forces (fauj) in hand, was better than a degree in the bush.

She could have been so many things, and who knows, maybe she would have liked to do more with her life. But she had ended up becoming a wife, and our mother. All the same, she was happy to have me out. She always told me how painless it had been for her to bring me into the world. I don't need to tell you that the law of averages has to catch up with all of us sooner or later. But she didn't expect that to happen. She even imagined that since I was a morning baby, I would have a calm temperament — another myth time would dispel quickly.

Her own mother had been immediately informed that I had arrived. There were no celebrations there. In fact, for a while, no one knew that I had been born. Then my granny casually shared the news with my grandpa.

'That's wonderful. Congratulations on your second grandchild,' he said to her.

'What's so wonderful? It's a girl!' she replied.

All the Punjabis I met were obsessed with baby boys. Ironically, it was my father's contribution of the XY chromosome that had determined my sex, but it was a bummer for my mother's family! My brother was just nineteen months old when I was born. Although I temporarily had the youngest-child status, and that of the only girl in the family, both were lost to my baby sister who was born three years and ten months later. Thus, I ended up being one of three children, and suffered from what I call the 'Middle Child syndrome'. Those who are stuck in the middle will know what I mean. We are not the first-borns who do everything first — crap, teeth, burp, walk, run, eat, talk... and, we are not the last-borns, who will always be the youngest and the cutest.

Doting upon her one and only son (which is something that all Punjabi mothers do), growing up herself, keeping a good home, cooking the best meals, being a good-looking wife, and quickly churning out a third baby, all before she had turned twenty-four, meant my mother had no time for me. Life sucked. And my biggest complex as a child was that no one loved me.

Parenting too was something else those days. In most Punjabi families it was, and maybe still is, mostly about two things: the kids must look good, and they must be well fed (read fat is healthy). They do sound like perfectly logical parameters to judge the well being of one's offspring, don't they? And, I suppose going by these parameters I had a wonderful upbringing, because I was chubby and fair. Now, we do love the colour white, don't we? My mother paid a great deal of attention to how well dressed I was. She was also protective — picking a fight or two for me before my sister was born. After she arrived, I was dethroned from my position.

I was incredibly jealous. I missed the attention, and I did all sorts of things to get it. I think my parents attended to most of my other needs, but they never realised that I had emotional needs as well. How does a four-year-old try to explain this to adults? Small things bother small children. If I cracked a joke, or accomplished anything noteworthy, it would be retold to the world with my brother on the credits list.

'But *I* did that, not *him*,' I would protest.

'Well done! Do you want a medal?' my mother wielded sarcasm well.

Hello? Did anyone notice anything I did at all? I mean, I might as well not have existed. How about some reverse psychology?

Soon I was failing in class, stealing from other students, and fighting with other kids. When I was nine, I even broke a classmate's wrist. Can you imagine *that*? Now whose parents would tolerate that? Then, I once told our neighbours that my parents didn't love me, and the word got around to my parents. It was very embarrassing for them, but they were careful to point out to me that I was well fed and well dressed, and therefore loved.

One day I asked my father, 'Will you be sad if I died?'

'That's a stupid question and doesn't deserve an answer,' he responded. Maybe if he had said yes, it would have been a sign that he loved me. Maybe he himself was finding it difficult to cope with a daughter who was absolutely not what he had expected! And, children don't come with a 'returnable' or 'exchangeable' policy.

My mother had even fewer ideas about how to deal with me. She tried everything she knew — thrashing, detention, lock-up, and the very famous stand-with-your-face-to-the-wall! I was punished every other day. My school would send for my parents. After a point my mother refused to respond to the summons.

'Tell your school principal I refused to come because you are so terrible that you cannot be my child,' she finally said.

So, I was not their child!

This was the time I established my relationship with God. That one didn't start off very well either. I remember many debates with my parents on the subject. I would offer the views of an atheist that made my parents uncomfortable. They couldn't figure out how they had managed to produce a child who didn't even believe in God. They would try to convince me that God existed. But, I suppose each one of us has to find our own God.

He is a clever chap, God. He had given me abundant talent for 'getting into trouble', and left no doors open for me to get out. So when I was very worried about the consequences of my misdeeds, and had no one to turn to, I would pretend I was talking to him on the phone: 'God, please help me, I just broke someone's wrist,' or, 'I just flunked my Sanskrit exam, so please save me from getting thrashed today,' or, 'I cut mom's favourite dupatta to shreds.' I think he did listen to my prayers. Almost always the consequences were softer than what I had imagined. Maybe he does exist after all.

I also learnt to trust God as I grew up. Once I prayed that he should make good-looking Ms. Molly my class teacher. I had thought she would be gentle, loving, and kind. He did make her my class teacher, but she turned out to be strict and nasty, and our class was caned every other day.

After one such caning session I called her a 'bitch', not to her face of course (that would have been suicide), but amongst my friends in class. Some smart-ass trying to get brownie points, sneaked on me to her. Now I was in even more trouble.

Whose fault was it? Who asked for Ms. Molly as my class teacher? Thus, I decided that I should leave my prayers alone and rely on Him to do the best for me, rather than ask for particular things, only to realise later that I had asked for the wrong things. So, although I don't have a real spiritual philosophy, and most people consider me spiritually demented, I have always felt very complete in my relationship with God.

I did not restrict him to a room or a corner in a temple, and my hotline meant that I could call him anytime and I would be attended to on a priority-basis like a Jet Privilege Platinum member. It was a good relationship and a consistent one.

Yes, I needed God because I loved to break all the rules. Luckily, my father was transferred somewhere new every couple of years, so we didn't have to put up with the embarrassment I generated for too long. But I was immune to my parents' problems with me. I had a great way to escape them. I was a dreamer, and lived in my own world, completely removed from my environment.

If only I could have done those things in my real life as well! Honestly, I always wanted to run away from home. I explored my options from time to time. When I was ten years old, and living at an Air Force station in a small village called Sarsawa, I seriously contemplated running away to Bombay to join the film industry.

Why that? I had heard my parents speak about the actor, Sunil Dutt. He was distantly related to us, and I wondered if he would take me in... you know, maybe launch me into an acting career as a child actor. I imagined all the things I could do and become if I ran away. Maybe I would find *some* acceptance. Of course, Sunil Dutt didn't know I existed in the first place. Maybe I could just ask for a job, any job, but I had no money to even buy a train ticket, and what if someone kidnapped me while I was on my way? I had heard stories of how bad people picked up kids and got them to beg if they didn't have any parents. I reassessed my situation. No, maybe hanging in here was better than running away. At least no one was going to make me wear rags and beg on the streets, and I would get three meals a day.

The years went by, but the thought of leaving home stayed with me. I am not so sure about how my siblings felt at that time, but they didn't seem to have too many problems. Neither my sister, nor my brother went through this stage of 'not fitting in', while I seemed to be permanently stuck there. My sister was, at that point, a nagging younger sibling, who tailed me all the time as I tried to shake her off. But, my brother — ah, he was something else.

I loved my brother. He was my parents' dream child. He would never get into fights, was a good student, as well as obedient and responsible. He was very much the sort of person who would abstain from airing his opinions, in case he got on anyone's wrong side. So you never knew if he agreed or disagreed with you. He was also the sort of brother who would never get into a fight to rescue me. Even later in life if I asked him for any thing, I could have it, but if I was in trouble and needed emotional support, he was not the one I could turn to.

I think he was also worried about spoiling his 'good boy' image with my parents. And he was definitely a good boy! I especially loved him because he was my mother's favourite. If only *I* could have had that status! For her, he could do no wrong. But of course a lot of that was also because he was a boy — something I didn't understand very well when I was a child. So I always thought that if I tried to be like him, I too would become my mother's favourite.

For many years I just copied him. It must have been quite annoying for him, poor chap. I would play the games he played, and I did the things he did. I think that really bothered my father. This was also one of the main reasons I avoided my father most of the time. Whenever he found me alone, I had to suffer his lectures on how 'un-girly' I was.

'Why are you like this? Good girls mustn't whistle, it's not lady-like. It is very important for a girl to maintain a good image,' he said.

And, there were other things: I mustn't laugh too loudly, I mustn't fight with the boys, and I must cross my legs when I sit! Oh lordy lord! Thankfully, my father had not heard the bad words I used outside the house, otherwise there was a pretty good chance that I would have realised my run-away dream immediately. My father was a gentle and loving parent and, to me, he was also quite boring.

One of the biggest perks of my father's work was that we were part of fauji campus life from the day we were born. We were protected from the outside world, within the boundaries of Air Force stations, amidst very tight security. Campus lives are typical. About thirty to forty families live together, and that makes it a very close-knit community. There is a distinct camaraderie, a brotherhood based on the deep-rooted know-ledge that we were all families of soldiers — in times of war and even in peace! Everyone knows everyone else, and everyone also knows *about* everyone else. Life's never without excitement, but ironically, most of the time life is also very predictable. It is a secular, cosmopolitan lifestyle.

We celebrated everything with equal enthusiasm — be it Christmas, Diwali, Eid, Holi, even birthdays and wedding anniversaries of people who didn't matter. New brides of officers were inducted ceremoniously by his fellow officers with pranks, followed by parties. The social calendar was choc-a-bloc. There was something about fauji kids — we were put through some invisible discipline and exposure that honed our personalities. We had to acknowledge every adult with a 'Good Morning' or 'Good

Evening' and be ready to respond if the other person wanted to strike a conversation. We were expected to be dressed impeccably to suit every occasion. We had to know our table manners! I could go on, but I think it's fair to say that generally speaking we were just whipped into shape... and style!

And, though we were not exposed to many things that ordinary citizens in 'civilian' life take for granted, we were privy to many privileges. We frequently interacted with the who's who — famous singers or actors who came to the Air Force stations to motivate frontline soldiers, war-heroes like Field Marshal Sam Manekshaw, and even India's first astronauts Ravish Malhotra, and Ravi Sharma (in the Air Force we considered them equal, though only one of them went into space), Chiefs of the Armed Forces and many others.

One day, we were allowed to skip school so we could meet a certain VVIP who was transiting through our Air Force station. My father was commanding the station and so we had even more liberties. Thus, my brother, my sister and I accompanied my mother to the helipad to greet the Prime Minister of the country. And, that was how we met Mrs. Indira Gandhi!

In the mid '80s, just before I turned thirteen, my father was posted to Bangalore. The city became our home for the next few years. While my parents found it increasingly difficult to deal with their problem child, the campus gave me a chance to find many friends and acceptance from some of my parents' friends.

One of my father's colleagues was a close friend. He accepted me better than any adult in my family. He lived in our neighbourhood with his wife and baby boy. I was often allowed to stay at their place during weekends. I loved going to his place because no one passed any judgements on me. To him and his wife I was just fine the way I was. They didn't care if I hadn't combed my hair, or if I didn't know how to peel a potato. They were not my parents to feel responsible for my failures. My situation with my parents was so desperate that several times I asked him to adopt me. Every time I did that, he would ask me why I wanted to be adopted.

What do you expect a confused teenager to say? I didn't even understand my circumstances myself, leave alone explain them to someone else. I was neither a child, nor an adult; it was such a bummer! And, bitching about my parents seemed like betrayal. After all, they brought me into this world. They had cleaned me, fed me, educated me, clothed me and, who knows, maybe in some ways they also loved me. The least I owed them was to say good things about them. Plus, I suspected that my not feeling loved could be a personal deficiency. Maybe it had nothing to do with my parents at all. Maybe it was all in my head. So I always stopped right there, and said, 'I would love to be your daughter.'

But life can never be all bad. There were also several good things about the way we were brought up. I can say that my parents were broad-minded in certain ways. We could wear what we wanted, no matter how short the shorts were, or how skimpy the tops. We were encouraged to be independent, and could make our own choices to a great extent. My brother, sister, and I were sent to the same school, so there was no visible discrimination.

Yet, there were things that didn't match up sometimes. I understood from family gossip that girls were expected to be virgin brides, while for boys it was an added qualification to have bedded lots of women. A girl with a drink or cigarette in her hand was cheap, while a man with one was cool. Despite an accomplished career, a girl ultimately had to prove herself by being home before the man, holding a glass of water for him when he came back from work. If there was dust in any corner of someone's house, it was a sign that the lady of the house was doing a bad job. Throughout my life I heard several such 'good-girl' rules that obviously never applied to my brother.

At home some things were exclusively available to my brother, and some jobs reserved only for my sister and me. It would immediately spark an argument between my mother and me. It was these things that made me defiant and rebellious, and I have to admit that I am stuck with these dumb qualities for life.

Whether I turned into such a person because I didn't have my parents' acceptance, or whether it was the other way round — I don't know. The answer probably lies somewhere in between. But rebellion was sweet. Inspiring. Motivating.

Chapter 2

I hung around with my brother and his friends all the time. By the time I was fifteen, all the girls I knew were playing games like badminton or table tennis, and cycling, whereas I was on the football field — always the single girl in a team of eleven. I played awfully, but I was still allowed in the team.

As a result of this, at fifteen, I had not a single girl friend. Most of my friends were boys on the football field. Yet, although I played with them, I was never really one of them.

Then came along Nicky, the cool dude. Nicky was new to our campus. He had spent a few years in Paris, and then lived in Delhi for a year before moving to Bangalore. That explained his high style quotient. He was the only boy who had a tuft on his head — the George Michael hairstyle of the mid '80s. He was the first person I knew who had a bicycle with gears.

A couple of days after we played football together for the first time, I saw him at school. He was in my Math class. His reputation preceded him. In a world where teenagers were discovering the existence of sex, here was a boy who had been there, done that. At first, people told me that his nickname was 'rapist'. I had heard him being called that by the other boys on the football field. So one day, while we were waiting for our Math teacher to come to class, I asked him, 'Why does everyone call you rapist?'

'I don't know,' he said.

'Maybe because you raped someone?' I offered cheekily.

'Do I look like someone who would rape anyone?'

I took a good look at him. Nicky was just five feet seven inches tall. He was thin, scrawny in fact, had light brown hair, and his crooked teeth peeked out when he smiled. He was an Aries. To me he didn't even look like someone who would kiss a girl forcibly.

'Actually, you don't. Still, there must be a reason why they call you that.' I wasn't going to let go.

'Well, the girls I slept with were willing, so that does not qualify as rape.'

Just then the Math teacher walked in. My brain stopped working. Damn! This boy who looked like a kid and *was one* had actually had sex. We were just fifteen years old. No way! I didn't hear a word of what the teacher said during the next forty-five minutes. I couldn't get over the shock. I had not even seen a man naked yet — not even a picture — and this boy, sitting next to me, had actually had sex with girls! Three girls apparently! I needed to know more.

The minute the class got over, I pounced on him.

'So where did you find these girls?'

'They were my classmates in Delhi.'

'You mean you had sex with girls who were like… our age?'

'What's so shocking about it? People younger than us have sex these days.'

Oh.

Then I couldn't afford to appear so shocked. I had to try and behave as if I had known all along that all this stuff happened. So I tried to act as normally as possible, but it was a bit too late. He knew I was going dizzy with curiosity.

'So where did you do it?'

'Wherever we got the chance — in the car, or at her place, or mine when our parents were out.'

We were walking home from school and he was talking as though it was the most ordinary thing for him to do. I imagined him having sex secretly with one of the girls at his home, while his dad walked in accidentally. I started to laugh.

'What's so funny?' he asked.

'Nothing. It just amuses me. You know, I don't know anyone else who is not a virgin.'

'You do know them, but you just don't know that they have been having sex too.'

This was even more shocking.

'You mean the boys, right?'

'Yeah, I only know the boys as of now. If I knew any girls, I would be sleeping with them,' he laughed.

'What sort of values do these girls have, sleeping around with boys just for fun? What about marriage?'

Of course, *that* came from all the brainwashing I had gone through in a Punjabi home.

'What about it? I am fifteen years old. Do I look like someone who can get married right now? All this 'values' business is in *your* head.'

I had never met anyone like him. He was being blatantly honest. He did exactly as he wanted to. He truly didn't care what anyone else thought of him. And he didn't do anything to please anyone but himself.

This, of course, was very different from my brother, who either did things to please my parents, or when he sensed a conflict, ensured that my parents didn't have the slightest idea about what he had been up to. I loved Nicky's openness.

My parents had been updated with the gossip, and my mother had already reprimanded me for hanging around with Nicky because he was a 'rapist'.

'He has a bad reputation. Everyone says he's raped two girls in Delhi. Not only should you avoid his company, you should also be careful, as a girl, about who you hang around with. People will start talking.'

I wanted to tell her that there had been three, not two, girls, but I didn't want to add to her agony. However, I neither stopped being friends with him, nor tried to hide the fact.

I told him about my conversation with my parents, and we both laughed over it.

'I love your bicycle,' I said.

'You can have it anytime you like.'

And just like that he would share anything I wanted. He was so easy-going.

One day I didn't see him at school. I went over to his place. He was running a fever. I walked right into his bedroom, and sat down on his bed.

'You need to stop being a wimp, and get out for some fresh air. Let's go for a walk,' I said to him. His house was right next to the golf course. All one could see for miles was green lawns dotted with trees.

'Go ahead. I will step out in a minute,' he said.

'No, I am waiting for you — right here,' I bullied him, waiting for him to get out of bed and wear his slippers.

'Can I wear some clothes, if you don't mind? I am naked under the sheets.'

So we were *The Wonder Years* buddies. He was the first guy I went out with for a drive, to a concert (his girlfriend was singing in it and it was simply awful), to a pub… and I even went to my first jam session with him. He introduced me to Elton John's *Nikita,* and to Dire Straits. I was so glad that I hadn't listened to my parents. Eventually, he became a frequent visitor to my house, and my parents accepted him as my friend. My mother even grew fond of him.

Though Nicky and I never talked about it, we had another thing in common. We were both misfits in our homes. He too had a difficult relationship with his mother. I had seen them fight a lot of times.

Nicky had many girlfriends during those two years in school. He fell in and out of love all the time, and we always gossiped and made fun of his relationships. From time to time, just to entertain ourselves, we would make a list of all the girls he had kissed or slept with, and all the boys I had a crush on. His list was always longer than mine. And by no means was my list ever short!

Chapter 3

Oh yes, I had many crushes — some that lasted a few hours, some a few days. With officers posted in and out of the camps, there was no dearth of new guys on the football field. One of them was Saiff.

He had arrived on our campus a few months after Nicky, and he occasionally played football with us. When most of us were in the thirteen to seventeen age group, he was twenty-five. He looked a lot like Imran Khan, the Pakistani cricketer (and the most eligible bachelor) those days. But it wasn't just his looks. There was something attractive about the fact that he was older than all of us — you know, not like the other 'kids' I played with. Maybe he could 'rescue' me from my situation at home. I was dying for him to notice me. I tried several tricks, and even tried to improve my football.

Nicky and he knew each other already. They had been neighbours in Delhi, and were co-incidentally together in Bangalore again. That happens a lot in the fauj. Hanging around with Nicky gave me the chance to meet him more often; though I am pretty sure I left no impression on him. But I knew his schedule by heart. He was a trainee at a technology company. I knew what time he went to work, what time he came back, and where he went after that. Occasionally, he played football with the 'kids'. Yes, that would be us. And, at times, he came to the Officer's Mess to play billiards or pick up a book from the library. I made it a point to be present wherever I could see him.

I would raise my eyebrows in surprise every time and say, 'Hi. Fancy seeing you here!'

Twenty-five-year-olds have a definite advantage over fifteen-year-olds, but at fifteen, you do not know it. While I pretended that all these were chance meetings, in reality I was stalking him and he knew it. I was just short of carrying a tattooed message on my forehead that read, *I have a crush on you.*

He was very nice about it. He humoured me at times, and even took an interest in my life. One day, we were chatting on the steps of the library. He asked me a very profound question: 'So, what are you planning to do after school?'

We were fauji kids, and the thing about fauji kids is that if you want to make something of your life, it is in your hands. Rarely does one see any disparity in the standard of living in people in the armed forces. All fathers earn more or less the same amount of money, and therefore, there are no pretensions. What you see is what you get. And if we need to make something of our lives, us fauji kids, we've got to do it ourselves because we don't exactly have our dad's business to take over, or a huge venture capital waiting for us.

But I was still far from that stage in my life.

What was I really going to do after school? I tried to think of the most impressive answer I could churn out. But the truth was that I had been so busy doing silly things, that I had paid no attention to what I wanted to do in life. Somehow, I had assumed that I would never get to that stage of my life to worry about it. 'I don't think I will live beyond eighteen, actually,' I said trying to sound dramatic, 'so I haven't given it much thought.'

'Really?' he was amused at my response. 'Yes, it is a possibility. But what if you live up to twenty-five? Or even fifty?'

Oh damn! I did not like this conversation at all. Why do smart twenty-five-year olds have to ask questions that make you look stupid?

'What do you see yourself doing? Being a mother to a few kids? Spending your life in the kitchen chopping vegetables, cleaning noses, packing school boxes? Nothing wrong with it, there are many who spend their lives like that, and you could do that too. Of course, you still have the option of dying young.'

I think he added the last line just to tease me.

Well, if those were 'our' children, I wouldn't mind!

But this was not the right time to voice such a thought. I tried to look very serious, as though I was soaking in every word of wisdom.

'How are your grades at school, Gauri?' he asked. This was the worst question I could imagine.

'Top ten in class,' I lied, as I desperately wanted him to think that I had all the brains in the world. The truth was that my focus at school was on bossing other kids around, and making fun of my teachers. I had spent most of my life just scraping through to the next class.

When I passed tenth grade, I chose to study Commerce, only because it was my brother's subject. But, as I was growing older, my feelings for him were changing too. Maybe it was the hot-blood of adolescence. His status with my mother that I could never have, irked me. So I still wanted to do everything that he did — except that I wanted to do it better. And though no one noticed or cared about what I was doing, that was my only aim.

I steered my mind back to this very important conversation I was having with Saiff, worried that I might not appear smart enough.

'You and the other kids,' (now that was certainly a direct reference to me), 'you just don't know the opportunities that await you. You are all protected, like frogs in the pond. You can be anything you want to be. Have you considered which college you want to go to? Have you thought of getting out of this sleepy town of Bangalore to study?' (It was true those days) 'Open your mind and do something with your life.'

He seemed so, so, *so* smart! I had never met anyone like him my entire life. The more I listened to him, the more I felt he was the best guy ever. There couldn't possibly be anyone better than him. I loved him already. As I dreamt on, he popped a question. *The* Question.

'Have you ever been on a date, Gauri?'

'Never,' I smiled.

Reading my mind, he asked, 'Would you like to go on a date with me?'

If it were possible for teeth to fall out of one's mouth in excitement, mine would have. As I write this, I can imagine how dumb I must have looked.

'I would love that.'

'Great. So here is the deal. I'll take you out on your first date, but you have to be in the top three in your class.'

'It's a deal,' I grabbed the challenge.

Wow. I couldn't believe I was getting the chance to go on a date with Mr. Good Looking! My mind was racing. I thought about what I would wear, where we would go, whether I would have the chance to hold his hand, and what we would talk about. I was already imagining conversations on this date that had not yet happened. Maybe one day we would be married to each other.

Except that the deal was that I needed to be in the top three in my class.

Now, a bit about Capricorns — the zodiac sign I was born under. When we want something, we figure out how we can get it, and put everything behind that goal. And my handsome, adult carrot at the end of the stick was worth everything. I wanted that date badly, and had only two months to make it happen!

I studied day and night and cut down on my fooling-around time, leaving myself with just enough free time to see Saiff once in a while. It was the same conversation every time we met:

'I am working towards that date, you better be ready for it.'

'You bet I am!'

Exams started and ended without incident, and the results were announced.

Saiff and I saw each other at the football field after a game.

'So what did ya think — would I top my class or not?'

'How did you do?'

'I didn't top my class.' I paused. 'I topped my school.'

It was true. I had been so devoted to my ambition that I had beaten all records. It was shocking, even to me. I had no idea that I had it in me to get there. As my grades improved, my life changed. Can you believe that a date changed my life? At school I was a star — a dark horse now.

And, for some reason, I also became the favourite child at home. I have never been able to figure out how that happened, but it did. It was an about-turn from problem-child to superstar, from zero to hero. All for the sake of a date with Saiff! Yeah, talk about the power of love, even if it is puppy love!

'That's wonderful! Good job. I knew you could do it.'

His appreciation was genuine and sincere.

'So when do we go on our date? Where are you taking me?' I wanted to get to the point.

'Soon. Maybe next month, after my pay day.'

Next month? Sounded like a lifetime. I needed instant gratification for such hard work, it had been an accomplishment. *But if I push him too much, I may appear desperate,* I thought. *But I am desperate.*

I tried to hide my disappointment, and managed to say, 'Sure, whenever you are free.'

Chapter 4

It was as if Saiff had re-aligned the stars for me, and opened my life to a new world. Suddenly, I had something else going for me too. Our school had a huge playground that was lined with trees. When the sunlight was too harsh, girls sat under the shade of these trees, but the hot sun never bothered the boys. Or me.

This afternoon, my Math teacher was standing under the tree, watching us play. Two teams were on the field — eleven boys in one team, ten boys and a girl in the other. After the game, he called me. I was sure I was in for a lecture.

'Why are you playing football?' he asked me.

Most girls in my class indulged in profound discussions about who had started their periods, and who had not, how dramatic their first period was, and the best sanitary pads to use. Or they wanted to discuss who the best looking hero in Bollywood was. Ah, now don't underestimate my love for gossip. But this was not the sort of gossip I enjoyed. I played with the boys in my class because I wanted to play with *someone* when the girls were chatting.

But I was not going to give the teacher this detailed explanation. I gave him a simple response, 'I like it, sir.'

I was surely gonna get it now. I thought he would say that it was a boys' game, blah blah blah...

'Has anyone told you that you play football like a donkey?'

Swear to God, those were his exact words!

'Actually, no sir.'

I have never been able to figure out if he was giving me a compliment or trying to make fun of me. At least a comparison to a more intelligent animal would have been less insulting.

'Have you ever tried athletics?'

'As in running?' I asked.

'No, field athletics... like throws, maybe discus or javelin?'

'I haven't. Too much hard work!' I laughed like a jackass, so maybe the donkey comparison was now justified.

'Well... no pain, no gain,' he said with a straight face. 'I want to see you here tomorrow after school. You have a powerful kick, but you play football terribly. You should be doing other things instead of wasting time over that.' He walked away.

Wasting time? I loved playing football!

This man was crazy. School got over at ten past three. And now I had to see him on the field when the sun was relentless, and it was hot like hell. Now the sun suddenly began to bother me as I talked to myself. Anyway, I did not dare not showing up. He was my Math teacher, and I would have to face him again and again.

So I stayed back after school, and he tried me out. He made me throw every damn thing he could lay his hands on.

He was not thrilled, but he was somewhat impressed — just a teeny-weeny bit. And I was stuck. He wanted to train me to be a part of my school athletics team. My event was going to be javelin throw.

Tell me, who ever goes to watch athletes throw javelins? Why couldn't he pick me for something a bit more glamorous? It wasn't even something the boys threw!

Now, I had to practise every evening after school for an hour. He kept a close watch on me, and worked very hard himself. He gave me videos to watch at home, and he was there every single day as I practised in the hot sun — watching me, teaching me, pushing me. And he was not even my sports teacher!

I am trying to avoid telling you about what happened to my date with Saiff. Well, days turned to weeks, and weeks into a couple of months. This much-awaited, to-die-for event in my life *never happened*!

One day I found out through Nicky that Saiff had a girlfriend — a real girlfriend — someone closer to his age. My heart broke into a million pieces. I was sure I would never recover from the loss of such divine love. But, strangely, it took only another cute guy on the football field for my heart to be Fevicol-ed back into its original shape.

Saiff had come into my life for a reason, and that reason was not to take me out on a date; it was to give me hope, to inspire me. Without him, I would never have tasted blood. He made me a marks-scoring lioness in the jungle of the school.

Chapter 5

One afternoon, before my last year at school started, I was returning home after playing Holi with my football friends when we were tempted by a sight that was impossible to resist — a squeaky clean girl on the streets. I was nudged to take the lead, and in a matter of minutes, we had dumped her in a pond — especially chosen for the tadpoles that bred in it. Gillian had arrived on our campus only the day before, and her family was still staying at the Officers' Mess. She was trying to make friends, but after that incident, she swore that she would never be friends with me no matter how starved for company she was. But there is a good reason why people say, 'Never say never'.

A few days later we became neighbours, and as soon as school reopened, we were in the same class and section.

Soon we were walking to school together, exchanging homework, and studying together. The rest of the time we would just 'hang around' with each other — no chasing footballs or bicycle racing, just 'hanging around'. Yet, doing nothing was the fun part — pouring out our high-strung adolescent emotions.

One weekend I stayed over at her place. We talked about her huge family back in Kerala. She had several cousins, all of whom she got along with and even loved. This was completely alien to me; I didn't even see my cousins every alternate year. Gillian and I went to sleep at an indecent hour that night after we had raided the fridge for a midnight snack. I woke up the next morning to find a note instead of Gillian next to me: 'Sorry, forgot about Sunday Mass. See ya later.' All I had to do was jump the fence to get home for breakfast. That was how my first sleepover ended.

By the time I turned sixteen — the perfect age to be in love — my academic and sports lives were on the right track.

Unfortunately, my love life was something else. At sixteen, everyone else around you has a girlfriend or a boyfriend.

But how does a tomboy, trying to trip boys during football, get that sort of attention from the same boys? I secretly admired Ryan, the tall and good-looking Anglo-Indian boy I had befriended on the by-now-famous football field. But one day he was really mean to me. He cut up my bicycle seat, poured Limca on it, and made me the laughing stock of the football gang.

So, the following day, I got to the football field earlier than him. I hid behind a wall, and waited for him to arrive and park his green Vespa. Luckily for me, he left his keys in the ignition, so that they wouldn't distract him when he was playing. He did not expect me to avenge myself. He probably underestimated me because I was a girl — a poor victim.

Hah, can you imagine that!

My operation was complete in a matter of seconds. I stuffed his petrol tank with sand, locked the scooter, and chucked his keys in the drain. I bravely left a note behind that read: DO UNTO OTHERS AS YOU WOULD HAVE THEM DO UNTO YOU. I even signed my name to prove my crime.

After that act of bravery, I turned…chicken. I didn't go to play football the next few days so that I would be safe.

Then, a week later, unexpectedly, he came over to my place to see my brother. He and I said nothing about the incident. Then he came again the next day. I told him my brother was not home. He sweetly said, 'I have come to see you.'

A few days later he passed me a love-note. That was the very first time a guy had ever told me that he loved me. And, even though a written note is not exactly the same thing as 'telling', I finally had a boyfriend, with a declaration of mutual love!

And, it was also very much one of those relationships you desperately want to forget after it's over. Most of these first loves are so embarrassing that when we look back at them, we end up asking ourselves the question that usually has no answer: *What the hell was I thinking?*

But it was a very exciting phase because I had never been through any of that before. It was a huge love affair that lasted all of seven weeks. He would pick me up from school and drop me home. We exchanged cards that were full of sweet nothings, and every time we were together we would hold hands. He was John Travolta from *Grease*. He even knew how to drive a car! And, with his looks, he was definitely a cool guy to hang out with. Oh, it is so easy to be impressed when you are sixteen — sweet... and stupid.

One fine day there was a kiss. This, at that time for me was the equivalent of having sex. And this is how he was now officially my boyfriend. Soon the word got around and there was nothing to hide.

He was enrolled in a college, but I noticed that he didn't seem very interested in getting himself any serious education.

He was of course a trendy guy, but without any ambition. Each day was what he wanted it to be, or most of the time, whatever I wanted it to be. I was in the final year in school. That year, a college listing had placed Sri Ram College of Commerce (SRCC) in Delhi as the best college in India; and Sydenham College of Commerce and Economics in Bombay, where my brother was studying, as the second best. Obviously, in keeping with my competitive spirit, I wanted to go to SRCC in Delhi because it was a notch higher than where my brother was studying. I knew that I would be competing with students from the entire country, many of them smarter than me.

I started to evaluate where this love affair was taking me. Did I foresee any future at all with this guy? What did he want in life? And, whatever it was he wanted, was it good enough for both of us to think of a future together?

Capricorns would rarely waste their time on anything meaningless. I had just been with him for a couple of weeks when all these questions started mushrooming in my mind.

One day I simply asked him, 'What do you want to become, Ryan? What do you want to do with your life?'

'Why do we have to talk about these things?'

'Look, I like to have fun, but I can't spend my entire life just playing football or watching you do bike wheelies. It's good to have an aim in life. Wouldn't you like to do something more with yourself?'

'Why are you lecturing me like my mother? I love you, and you love me, and that is all that there is to this. Why are you worried about the future? I will do whatever makes you happy.'

So you see, he was not just my boyfriend, he was also my own lamp-genie.

What choice did it leave me? Though I was just sixteen, it was not at all confusing. I was learning my first lesson in love, and it was a lesson about respect. Respect, even for the self, came from having some goals. It came from doing something. It didn't matter whether it was something that got you money, or fame, or just plain satisfaction. I wanted Ryan to *be something*.

By now I was the head girl in school. In addition to sports and studies, I was also managing a boyfriend who was a lost eighteen-year-old. Ryan drank and smoked occasionally, and I wondered if he was a bit young to be doing these things. Soon I started meeting his friends.

I realised I had been like them until a few months ago... until Saiff had come along. But now I was on a different path.

I wanted to achieve something, while he and his friends didn't have a clue about what they wanted to do. I had the choice to go back to being like them. Or I could chug along the track I had recently shifted on to, which was hard work, but also one that gave me a real high. And, not to forget, the promise of a real future. Ryan's friends, Ryan himself, and I had the same opportunities. The difference lay in what we wanted to do with those opportunities.

There was another thing in this entire equation with Ryan — my parents. My mother simply could not believe that I had chosen this loser as my boyfriend. And now I also had her making my life hell. She stopped sending me to school because, according to her, I was using that as an opportunity to meet him. I was grounded, and assigned household chores like doing the dishes, sweeping, and mopping.

My parents had very little confidence in me. My mother was a strong and stubborn person, but she did not realise that, as her daughter, I could match her strength and iron will. And, I was smarter than she gave me credit for.

I didn't show up at school for three days. Then Gillian and Nicky came to see me. Gillian sat on the study table in my room, and Nicky sat on the bed, under watchful glances from my mother. Pretending I was asking them about what I had missed at school, I told them about the way I was being treated at home.

'What are you gonna do?' Gillian asked.

I smiled so that I would look brave, but tears were rolling down my cheeks. My mother had treated me so badly that many of the things that she said are unmentionable even today. Maybe she was trying to protect me; maybe it was socially embarrassing for her.

'I need to get the hell out of here! And for that I really need to get back to school.'

I hated my life at that point. I didn't feel it was my home. I wanted to flee, I felt desperate. I wanted to change my life. I had no idea how I would achieve that, but I saw an opportunity if I could get into a good college.

'You will get out.'

I knew Nicky and Gillian would help me.

My parents were fond of Nicky. Despite his extra-curricular activities with the fairer sex, he always did well at school. And they were thankful that I had befriended Gillian, at least a girl in my circle of friends, even if she was the only one.

Now, only I knew why I was under house arrest. My parents would not tell my friends because that would make them look bad. So Nicky asked my parents why I hadn't been going to school, pretending he didn't know.

'She knows why,' my mother replied. 'Hasn't she told you?'

'No, she hasn't,' he lied.

That made me look good. *Yes, I am wrong and you are right. Can we end this power struggle please?* I was too stubborn to do it, so here were Nicky and Gillian doing it for me.

'It's just that tomorrow is the inter-school sports competition, and the school needs her there. Our Math teacher has been asking about her every day because the school can't miss this chance.'

They spoke as if they were there on behalf of the school, and it was true in a way.

'Okay, I can send her if she agrees to abide by the rules. She knows what those rules are.'

It *was* a power struggle like I had guessed.

Should I give in?

I was sixteen years old, living in their house, spending their money. Did I have a choice?

I went to school the next day, and we went for the sports meet. My Math teacher accompanied me to the competition.

No other teacher, throughout my life, had left any impression on me. Maybe it was because I had little interest in school, or maybe the teachers had little interest in me. But he was a different kind of teacher. He came to school on a motorbike, and had hair streaked with silver, falling over his forehead all the way down to his glasses.

But that was not what made him special. He was extraordinary because he had not become a teacher to collect his pay cheque at the end of the month; he had become a teacher because he loved to teach. And, to him, teaching was not just about telling us the rules of trigonometry. He felt that his job was to help us recognise what we were capable of, beyond the marks we scored, and to motivate us to get there. And he had achieved that with many students. Now it was up to me.

He was helping me stretch and warm up, and like a coach, he kept babbling motivational speeches. Of course he knew nothing of my situation at home, or with Ryan, but he said something that made sense to me then, and remains in my mind even today.

'You know, the thing with athletics is that it's not a team sport. Here, you are the only one who matters, so you need to give it your best. Don't be afraid to want to win. If you win, treat your competitors with respect; they worked and tried as hard as you did. If you lose, walk with your head held high, with a smile on your face, and remind yourself that you did your very best.

Winning and losing are two sides of the same coin.'

Good or bad, I was competitive and loved a good challenge. In fact, ever since Saiff had shown me what I was capable of, I was always ready to put up a fight. Competition has facilitated our survival for thousands of years. If not for food and water, then for minerals, fossil fuels, land... we have been competing from the very beginning. Yes, I know many people who don't believe in competing, but not me. I always remember what my Math teacher told me that day, almost twenty-five years ago — it's not always about winning!

I won two golds. On the way back from the meet I fell inside the bus. My mouth hit the railing, and my front tooth was chipped. It's still broken, I never got it fixed. Yes, it's not related to my story, but it's good to have information, so I thought I would slip it in.

I went on to compete in the state levels, and then the regional, and the next, till I was finally at the Juniors' National Meet. I finished sixth at the nationals, with just a few months of training. It was my last year in school. So this was the best I could have done. My school was very proud of me, all thanks to one man. My parents were thrilled. They loved me again. At some level, of course, all parents love their children because we are an extension of them. But this style of giving me importance when I was a star, and shunning me when I was not one, was particularly annoying. I like consistency in my relationships. My relationship with my parents rarely had that.

No doubt you'd like to know what happened to Ryan. One morning after my inter-school sports meet I woke up, and bingo, the bubble had burst! I was someone who wanted to get somewhere, and he was someone who didn't even know where he was. I wanted to be with someone who was better than me. So I met him one afternoon and broke up with him.

At the cost of fast-forwarding the story just a bit, I need to add what became of Ryan. A couple of years later, he and his friends were at a party. They brought out a gun loaded with a single bullet to play Russian Roulette. The bullet went through a girl's head and blew her brains out. It was a terrible accident, but they all had serious criminal charges against them. Some boys even spent a few days in jail. I was God's child and God had shown me the way at the right time.

Chapter 6

Four months later, I wrote my final board exams.

While I waited for the results, during one of my visits to my favourite uncle's place, I met one of his colleagues — another pilot, just like my father and uncle, but younger than them. For years my father had taught scores of young men, such as my uncle, to fly planes. He now trained the next generation. Everyone in the Indian Air Force knew my father as one of the first few helicopter pilots in the country. So, although no one knew who I was, they all knew whose daughter I was. To them I was a SODA, a member of the Senior Officers' Daughters' Association! This young pilot, a good and responsible boy, and a Malayali, became my next boyfriend over the next few meetings.

A Punjabi girl and a Malayali boy — a girl as north Indian as she could be, and a boy as south Indian as possible.

Secretly, I have to be honest, I always despised being a Punjabi. I always tried to be as un-Punjabi as I could be, but I think in some areas I was very unsuccessful. Punjabis are loved for their culture, zest, and enthusiasm, but having lived in a Punjabi family, I had a different opinion.

I noticed that Punjabis had egos bigger than their cars, and even their homes. They loved to sweat the small stuff. They are more materialistic than any other community I know (at least all the Punjabis I know). Above all, even in the most modern of Punjabi families, there is discrimination (no matter how subtle) between boys and girls, and that really got my goat.

I mean look at my own granny's reaction when I was delivered to the world! Now, at this point I have to offer my profuse apologies to any Punjabi family that is not like this, but if you do exist, I would certainly like to meet you. Really!

Of course, I had no doubt that marrying a handsome Punjabi man (which without question almost all Punjabi men are), would also mean inheriting the excess baggage of a dominating mother-in-law. So I had made up my mind that I would never ever marry a Punjabi. Yes, I was guilty of this discrimination. I could do nothing about some of my Punjabiness, such as my fair skin, my love for chai, and maybe even my aggressiveness, but I tried to hide my roots with vague replies when people asked me if I was a Punjabi.

My parents evaluated every eligible Punjabi boy as a suitable match for me, but I would have none of it. I had carried my personal ban on Punjabis so far that I realised I didn't even have any close Punjabi friends, leave alone boyfriends!

Just when I started romancing this young man, my board exam results were declared. Nicky had done well, and he had no trouble getting himself a seat at a good engineering college. He stayed on in Bangalore. I had done very well too, and was confident that I would get through SRCC in Delhi — *the* college for commerce. The day before I was leaving Bangalore, Saiff came home to say goodbye.

That was odd, wasn't it? I thought so too.

Obviously, I wasn't expecting him. I don't know if he came to make up for the date that never happened, but he was still going out with the girl at his office. He even brought me a farewell gift — a lovely garnet necklace — because that was my birth stone. Maybe he did have some interest in my life after all.

I left Bangalore. I don't think it was very easy for my parents to send me to a college outside Bangalore. My father had retired a year ago. I knew he had lost a lot of money after that. He had chosen to trust someone, and been taken for a ride. It was very tough on him.

Rewinding to a few decades earlier, the India-Pakistan Partition of 1947 was my father's riches-to-rags story. Like millions of Hindus, he had migrated from Rawalpindi to India as a refugee when he was eleven years old. He was sixteen when he joined the National Defence Academy. By nineteen he was training to become a pilot, earning his own money, and giving some to his parents. I think he might have liked to become a doctor — and he would have made a very good one — but that would have meant studying for more years, and being a financial burden. So he chose a career that would help him earn.

He had worked all his life to save for the future, and now it was gone. Having flown planes for over thirty years, he had no expertise or the will to do anything else. The three of us were still studying. Funding our education was a huge burden for him.

My mother had been born three years after the Partition. I think she had always been more ambitious than my father, except that she had no real career herself, but like all parents who have not achieved their own goals, she hoped that her children would have a career and study more than she had. She was ambitious for us. This was one of the many incongruities that cluttered her mind, because this also contradicted one of the good-girl rules. I believe she would have been equally happy if we had married rich men, and done nothing in life.

Anyway, it was her, the more worldly wise, and not my father who accompanied me to Delhi to help me with college admissions. College admissions are a circus, and the applicants the clowns. We waded through queues, and lists, and forms.

Oh, how we ooze with confidence when we are frogs in our ponds. Only when we step outside do we realise that there are thousands of outstanding frogs croaking all over the world!

I didn't get admission to SRCC. Can you beat that? After all the pompous declarations of all my achievements, I didn't make it. The cut-off was one per cent higher than my score. Between my grades and the cut-off score were hundreds of other students. Even my achievements in sports was not enough.

I was offered a seat in Economics. So, I would end up in the same college, but not with the subjects I wanted. I needed to think about it. I can't even remember now why I was so stuck up about

Commerce, because come to think of it, Economics is a great subject too. Time was running out. Most colleges were closing admissions. I would end up with no seat at all if I did not make up my mind.

My mother and I headed home. That day I experienced what hundreds of girls in Delhi go through every day. I was eve-teased by a man who looked old enough to be my father, and so very decent!

I didn't know how to react. It was not the first time I had been physically abused, but it was the first time that it had happened in public. And even though I was not alone, it had happened so quickly that I had not been able to do anything. I started to cry, partly because I didn't know how to react, and partly because I was angry and disgusted.

That moment I told my mother I didn't want to live in Delhi. I would hate the city for the rest of my life.

Chapter 7

I had no clue about what I was going to do. Admissions had already closed in Bombay, but I was not going to live in Delhi. I had made up my mind. So we went to Bombay, and that is how the city became my home.

I know this city has been renamed Mumbai. I have no problem with anyone wanting to rename anything or anyone — barring me — except that, as a true Bombay girl, I find it difficult to call it Mumbai. It was Bombay when I landed there, and it has always been Bombay to me. No offence intended to any political parties in, or out of, power.

The first thing that struck me about Bombay was the sheer number of people, and the ease with which everyone mixed with everyone else. The chaos was so incredibly organised! There were entrepreneurs at every corner of this city — from the sandwich-wala, to the Aarey-milkbooth man. I had not seen any of these things before — the overflowing local trains, the black and yellow taxi, the silhouettes of huge, tall buildings with (ironically) tiny apartments, and people who had no time to stop as they were always running after an invisible Mr. Rabbit from *Alice in Wonderland*.

Although admissions had closed, my exceptional sports achievements helped me get into Sydenham College — the one my brother was studying in. I thanked God for giving me the love for football, for giving my Math teacher the opportunity to watch me play, for giving him the strength to deal with an athlete who had the concentration span of a lizard, and for giving me the chance to go all the way to the nationals. When I was still a child, my mother had told me that there would be many situations in my life when God would show Himself to me. This was one of those times.

I moved to a hostel. It was a government hostel, and was not attached to any particular college. My mother left after I had settled into my new home. I went to see her off at the train station with my brother. It was bustling with people.

There were still a few minutes for the train to leave. My mother muttered a long list of dos and don'ts.

'Don't waste money. Don't eat junk food. Don't waste time. Study hard. Be careful with money. Eat an egg every day. Make sure you drink two glasses of milk. Soak five almonds before going to bed, and eat them first thing in the morning.'

This list of dos and don'ts has always remained the same. As I made more friends at the hostel, I discovered it was a standard list with all mothers. Barring a few substitutes here and there, the advice from all of them was identical and unimaginative.

The train blew a warning whistle. She gave me a tight hug. It was not just an act of affection; it was as though she was trying to tell me that she loved me. As long as I had lived at home, I could never make out if she did. It was the tightest hug I had ever got from her. Her voice started cracking as she gave my brother orders to look after his kid sister. She climbed into the train, but stood at the door. I could see her furiously wiping away her tears as her train chugged further away from us. I was misty-eyed, but didn't cry. On the contrary, I tried to lighten the atmosphere with some dumb jokes.

And I was on my own now. Finally.

Life in the hostel was a contrast from life at home. And these three years of college were the only time in my entire life when I felt some sense of attachment with my home and family. I missed them terribly. It was during this time that my sister and I became close friends. We wrote letters very often — almost every week. I visited my parents often. I missed my mother the most. She and

I were very different, yet, in so many ways we were just the same. Though my brother and I saw each other almost every day at college, the first few months were very difficult.

I had arrived at Bombay with exactly one suitcase, and an incredible amount of excess baggage — of opinions — based on what I had seen in the seventeen years of my life. Many of them were incredibly daft. The world I had come from was completely different from this new world.

I didn't want to waste my father's money, so I made some rules for myself. I would never smoke a cigarette or buy myself a drink with his money. Actually, the first one was the easiest rule to follow because I never smoked a single cigarette all my life anyway, and I swear it had nothing to do with being a good Punjabi girl!

I also promised myself that I wouldn't waste my life. I tried to be responsible. The first few months I rarely went out partying — firstly because I hardly had any money, and secondly because I thought it would make me digress from my goals. I even got myself a part-time job after college hours so that I could make some extra money to travel.

It is a bug I've always had.

Chapter 8

At the hostel I was assigned a room with Riya. She came from a wealthy family. Although she was studying Interior Designing, I don't think she was terribly serious about her career. As a fauji kid, the first thing that struck me about her was her overflowing wardrobe. I remember spending most of my growing-up years with limited clothes, waiting for an occasion to get new ones.

Riya was slim, had spotless skin and large black eyes. She was about half an inch taller than me. And she was Ms. Popular. She had more friends than the clothes in her cupboard! Compared with the friends I had on the campus, Riya was exactly the opposite. I went through conflicting feelings. I was scared to have too much fun (justifiably, I assure you — we know of the Ryan episode).

Though there was nothing wrong with her, to me her big gang of friends, part-time college, and the habit of eating out every other day was shocking. I was a small-town kid who had just arrived in this big city. She was too polite to tell me that, but I am sure she must have found my moral lectures a pain in the butt!

I had been living with Riya for less than a month when, one day, she innocently asked me if I would like to go out clubbing with her and her friends. That was it. She was trying to make me like herself, and throw me off track! I made some lame excuse to decline the offer. As soon as she left, I started to cry. I felt like a lost and confused puppy on the street with no home or friends. I went to the hostel mess for dinner, and tried to shove some terrible-tasting grub into my mouth. My eyes were puffed up with all the crying, as the tissue paper lying next to my plate desperately tried to stay together.

Asha, a student at the JJ College of Architecture, was sitting at the other end of the dining table, watching the drama. 'Why have you been crying?' she asked directly.

'I want to change rooms. Do you know if someone else needs a room-mate?' I asked in a pathetic voice. I didn't need to beat around the bush either.

'In fact, I do know someone.'

As soon as we were done with dinner, most of which I could not get down my throat, given my emotionally imbalanced condition at that hour combined with the awful flavours, she took me to room number 407. The room was occupied by a senior student from her college who luckily didn't have a room-mate. I had no idea at that time that fate had led me to whimper at the mess so that Asha could introduce me to one of my greatest girl friends ever.

Room number 407 was a funky room, done up in a highly individual style. It had a huge poster of the Beatles (I didn't know who they were then), and lots of smaller posters of other crazy-looking people (apparently members of various rock groups). Against the wall was a very large table — bigger than most other tables I had ever seen. Later I would find out it was a drafting table that architects used. I was introduced to Rima. The minute I saw her, I started crying again.

Rima was a strong person. A tough cookie is what she was. She had long dark hair, all the way to her hips, and she sported a big bindi on her forehead. A faded block-print kurta gave her an ethnic look.

She was studying to become an architect. During her stay at the hostel she had seen a few 'kids' like me. She was four years older than me. She heard my story and told me I was free to move in with her if I liked, but she also told me that I was making a mountain of a mole-hill. 'What's wrong if she likes to party?'

'I don't know who she goes out with,' I sobbed.

'Grow up, woman! How does it matter?'

'I don't know what goes on at these parties.'

'How will you know unless you go and find out? No one can make you do anything you don't want to do.'

I started bawling even more loudly so that she would see how genuine my point was, but I don't think it had the desired effect. She shook her head in exasperation. The next day I became her room-mate.

Rima was something else. She was assertive, not someone who could be pushed around. She was extremely intelligent, and she knew much more about everything than I did, but she never made me feel stupid. She was always willing to get drawn into a debate, explain what I didn't know, and challenge my opinions.

Living with her, I started using my own brains and forming my own opinions. And, I learnt what architecture meant.

Until I had met her, I didn't know that a profession like that existed. Talk about ignorance!

She also introduced me to Ringo Starr and Paul McCartney — not literally, but she always did hang out with them in a way. They entertained her while she worked — and thus, I learnt about the Beatles. She taught me how to manage my money, how to put away for a rainy day, but keep enough to enjoy life.

At times she could be crude in a way that some hostelites are. She uttered the filthiest obscenities with perfect ease. She had the greatest vocabulary of bad words in several languages, and the largest collection of dirty jokes that she delivered with absolute finesse. She was worse than the boys on the football ground!

We had a guru-shishya, older sister–younger sister, and sometimes even bully-sissy, relationship. But she was very protective of me. Although she gave me a lot of lectures from time to time, she accepted me completely for what I was. That was not really something I had ever had in my life. Even my brother's girlfriend was always trying to tell me how I should behave. But Rima didn't ever tell me how I could be better, nicer, sweeter, or anything else-er. In fact, according to her, it was always an advantage to have a bit of evil in you.

'It is self-defence,' she would say.

She was my new Nicky.

Meanwhile, on the love-life front, I remained the girlfriend of the young officer — a very nice man. In the beginning, I liked this long-distance relationship. It meant that I had love in some little corner and a life of my own. But, after a few months, I discovered that I was not a long-distance relationship person. It seemed to be too much work, and the relationship didn't feel real either. It was like having an imaginary boyfriend.

We didn't see each other often enough, we were not there to support each other, and the relationship did not give me a sense of belonging. It works for some folks, but it didn't work for me. With time, we came up with some lame reason to break up. I suspect that I just got bored of a relationship built on too much letter writing. So, breaking up with this man was not very painful.

As with all my other boyfriends, my mother hadn't approved too much. Why? Well... because she was my mother, of course! Like in the case of careers, when it came to relationships, I don't think she was clear about the matter herself. She wanted to be 'cool', as in 'My daughters can have boyfriends', but often, when my sister and I told her about our boyfriends, she didn't really want to accept them unless they were rich Punjabi boys. My sister did have one like that, and he was the only one my mother loved.

She wanted us to have the freedom she had never had, but she didn't want to accept the consequences. She expected we would eventually settle down with boys of her choice. It was a bit hypocritical, I think, but then that's so totally Punjabi too!

Life went on and my philosophy during those years can easily be described in a Charlie Brown comic strip I once read. Charlie had been asked to write an essay on life and his was, 'Who knows!' When his teacher told him it wasn't long enough he rewrote it: 'Who knows, who cares!'

Chapter 9

The next year Riya and Asha moved into a room next to ours, and we became the 'girl gang'. There were so many things about Riya I had failed to see the first time we met because I was only looking at a single dimension. Now I saw her with 4-D vision. Ironically, I became the wild one in every conceivable way. Thinking about her once, it even struck me that she was probably the kind of daughter who would have made my father very happy. She was not a tomboy, she was obedient and respectful towards everyone's parents, and later in life she married a boy her parents chose for her.

She was my Florence Nightingale. Once when I had terrible food poisoning, Riya spent the entire night sitting next to me. I had vomited eight or nine times. By then, with an empty stomach, all that came out was a mixture of bile and blood. My head throbbed and I felt sick, but she was there — massaging my head, holding my hand — just like my father would when I was little.

'Go to sleep. You have college tomorrow,' I told her.

'You don't need to worry about that right now.'

The four of us became family to each other in a way that many hostelites do. We had responsibilities day scholars knew nothing of. And, there was a big factor that bound us together. The very important vitamin: money. My Accountancy teacher in school always told us that money was a real vitamin. What vitamins do to our body, money does to our lives (I think he might have said business, but I am taking the liberty to stretch that analogy here).

And we hostelites suffered from an acute deficiency of that vitamin. As birds of a feather, we flocked together.

The coolest day-scholars, at least in my college, were rich kids. Several were children of industrialists, celebrities, and famous politicians, who would go to international universities from here, where the fee for a year of education was what my father had earned in his entire life, maybe more.

They came to college in chauffer driven cars — each fancier than the next — while we commuted by bus or train, and towards the end of the month we walked to get anywhere!

They had their own social circle, and partied at places such as 1900s the nightclub at the Taj, while the favourite social haunt of the hostelites was the college canteen. And when there was a really special occasion, we ate chocolate ice-cream. Of course, we did go to the iconic Taj Mahal hotel occasionally, to use their bathroom, because that was the only thing that was free.

One day, we had an Orchid Auction in college. I remember a girl from my class, who bought orchids for her boyfriend, for an amount of money that equalled my spending allowance for three months. It took me a whole week to get over the fact that her father had actually given her that sort of money, and that there would be no questions asked.

She threw a party to celebrate the fact that she had bought the orchids. Even more spending! She invited us to her home at Cuffe Parade, one of the most upmarket areas in Bombay. Let's be clear. We were not there as friends. But a successful party that would be talked about for days must have a crowd. How else would it look popular? So we all went for it.

She lived in a penthouse that had a terrace. I had never seen such a glitzy house in my life. The black marble flooring was shiny enough to reflect even the colours of our *chaddis*! The drapes were exquisite, and there was expensive China and Belgian cut-glass in every corner. I was so worried I would knock something over that I stayed on the terrace almost all evening.

The bathroom was even jazzier than the one I had seen in the Taj, and it was stocked with beauty products that I had never seen — enough to start a beauty salon. For food, they served the best Thai cuisine, and the drinks flowed.

Back at home, even my last birthday had been celebrated with balloons and a cake. I could not comprehend how this girl, who was my age, had the money to throw a party, the expense of which exceeded my entire year's expense; and her parents didn't even care who attended this party. We all had fun together, and then everyone went home. No discussions, no bringing out problems, no bonding. That was how most of our relationships with day-scholars were.

Frankly, after all that excitement and euphoria about going to college, it was a bit of a disappointment. School had been intimate and fun. College was huge and impersonal. The only good thing was that it had an excellent reputation, so the smartest kids came here, and that gave me a chip on my shoulder. Beyond that, it was totally uninspiring. I came from a school that had huge playgrounds. The college had huge space constraints. It was an old colonial building, but was still just a block of cement. Most of the students had already been studying here since junior college, so the cliques were already formed. I had joined in senior college. Though I was friendly, I had very few day-scholar friends.

Jigna and Hiten were in my class. Jigna and I stayed at the same hostel, while Hiten was in the boys' hostel where my brother stayed. They were a good-looking couple, and had known each other since junior college. I hung around with them in the college canteen, usually jabbering some non-stop nonsense, passing snide remarks on sundry day-scholars.

They both were very sober, and thus very different from me. They said that I was entertaining company.

Most of the things I did — like taking off to Goa on my own one weekend without telling anyone, gate-crashing at parties, kissing my boyfriends in public, etcetera, were things they could not ever dream of doing in their lives. I have to say that I did my best to inspire them, but I failed most of the time.

Jigna was an outstanding student. She was useful for borrowing college notes the day before the exam. She was smarter than Hiten, if we judged her only on the basis of exam scores. But she didn't come from a family that put any pressure on her to become anything. I suspect she had been sent to college only to improve her value in the marriage market. Even men, who want their wives to be confined to the kitchen, look for women who have some education. But Hiten was different. He had varied interests. His thirst for learning, competing, and improving was never satiated. He read weird books — he was always borrowing library books on psychology, automobile mechanics, the Holocaust, Einstein's theories (that one was incredibly boring), and even criminology. He knew more about the stock exchange than any other person our age. He was an excellent orator, played the drums, and loved a good debate (naturally, I avoided getting into one with him). He was not someone you could ignore.

Jigna's short-term goal was to know all she needed to know about Accountancy, so that she could score a distinction.

In the long term, she limited herself to one ambition — to get married to Hiten and raise his children.

They had been 'engineered' to fall in love. That meant if you knew a relationship could culminate in marriage, you used that as a basis to allow your feelings to develop. First, you matched your family backgrounds (they were both Gujaratis), next the religion, parents' financial status, and so on. Hundreds of love marriages are arranged like this.

They were just a few months apart in age, and there was no objection from either family when they declared their love for each other. A completely boring love story, if you ask me: boy and girl meet and fall in love. There is no drama, no elopement, no controversies. Everyone accepts everyone, and they were to be married as soon as they graduated from college!

'You are so young. How can you be sure you want to marry this guy? I mean... I like Hiten, he is a great guy, but he is the first guy you have ever known,' I said to her one day. I was already on boyfriend number four by then.

'My mother too married the first man she saw.'

'Yeah, so did mine, but that was more than two decades ago.'

'I am just lucky that I can marry someone I love. Most girls in my family will never have the chance to marry a boy they like.'

By the time I moved to the second year, my life had changed a lot.

Let us not forget that one man who had made it possible. What was I doing with life before I fell flat for Saiff?

Saiff and I never exchanged letters. After all, you may have realised, that we had *nothing* — as in nothing at all — going on. But, in a moment of overpowering emotion, with gratitude taking control of my right hand, I penned a letter to him thanking him for changing my life. He replied very modestly, telling me that it was my hard work that had done it.

A fast forward here is necessary. Three years after I had completed college, our paths crossed again — in Delhi. Nicky had moved there, and we were out for ice-cream when Saiff drove past us. He stopped his car because Nicky waved to him. We all stepped out of our cars.

'It's great to see you,' I said. We had not seen each other for six years.

He looked at me and smiled.

Then most politely he said, 'You know, I know I know you, but I simply can't place you. Tell me, how do we know each other?'

It didn't matter. Life had moved on and, like I said, he had justified his existence in my life.

Chapter 10

Nicky and I stayed in touch. We were not the type to write to or call each other, but I visited Bangalore often and we always met. His father had been transferred back to Delhi, and he started spending his vacations there. Those days I had to put up with excruciatingly long descriptions of his new girlfriend Sheeba. He was crazy about her, and drove Gillian and me nuts talking about her.

Maybe she was his first true love. I thought he was mad because he was the same boy who at fifteen had told me he couldn't think of marriage when he was bedding all kinds of girls. And now, at nineteen, he was talking about having kids. She lived in Delhi, and he used every little opportunity to scuttle off to Delhi to be with her. Love was sobering him down. He was studying harder, and trying to make something of his life. Love does have that effect on some of us. I have to admit I had never seen him like that before. I was amused, but also impressed. Yet, I counted the days before this would change, and I let go of no opportunity to tease him about it.

It was around the same time that I met Shiraz in the college in Bombay. One day, I was drinking some 'cutting' coffee (half a glass at half the price) in the canteen when he walked in and sat down opposite me, because all the other seats were taken.

'May I join you?' he asked.

'What part of me looks un-joined?' I grinned. 'Okay, but only if I am going to get compliments. It is a day for me to feel good.'

'That's not difficult with a girl as cute as you.'

'Don't call me cute. Do you know the real definition of cute is "ugly but tolerable"?'

'That is exactly what I meant — like a toad.'

This nonsensical exchange continued for a while.

'So what do you do other than verbal fencing with strangers?' he asked.

'I try to pretend I am a student in second year, and get strangers to pay for my coffee.'

'I am a Parsi priest when I am not busy completing my assignments.'

I had never known any Parsis, leave alone a Parsi priest.

Now for a short history lesson on Parsis, also called Zoroastrians.

These folks immigrated to India from Iran in the tenth century and, over the centuries, they have integrated themselves in the country by adopting Indian customs and traditions, including language. They have retained some of their religious beliefs and created their own unique identity here. They are famous, amongst other things, for their eccentricities… to the extent that they have affectionately been labelled 'mad-bawas', with no offence intended to my long list of Parsi friends whose idiosyncrasies I love (after all, madness and smartness are two sides of the same coin).

They are one of the first communities to have produced women leaders in the corporate world in India. Amongst Indian Parsis, the sons of priests or any other member of their family can become priests by going through two grades of initiation, without having to give up their normal life. They can get married, have sex, produce children, and eat what they like just as all other mortals do. Though Bombay is full of Parsis, there are less than a hundred thousand Parsis in the world, and a small percentage of them are priests.

Why have I told you this?

To make the point that I was rubbing shoulders with the rarest-of-the-rare.

Shiraz was an MBA student in the management college at Sydenham. It was 11.00 am when he asked me if he could sit with me and, before I knew it, it was 11.00 pm. That was curfew time at my hostel. I was having such a good time with him that I could have sat there the whole night chatting about silly, meaningless things. But it was Cinderella Time and I had to go, otherwise the mice would turn to pumpkins and I would be stranded outside with this guy all night and I didn't want that.

So we met the next day, and the next day, and the next. He was about an inch taller than me, and he and I actually looked like siblings. We had the same complexion, the same long nose, pointed chin, and if madness was a criterion, we were similar even there — of course since he was a Bawa, I was hardly any competition.

He was the first ever person to write a poem about me. It was funny, just like him. He would take me loafing everywhere on his motorbike. We went to all the places Bombay was known for — like the Hanging Gardens, and Tea Centre at Churchgate. It was with him that I went to Mondegar Pub — the only one that had a juke box those days, and to Britannia, famous for its Berry Pulao. We would walk down from one end of Marine Drive to the other. Though romance is not the word to describe our 'relationship', it was quite a romantic walk: from one end, you could see the lights in an arc that seemed to be strung like a yellow necklace. I finally learnt why they called it Queen's Necklace.

Then one day as he saw me off at the hostel gate, he bent forward and kissed me. It was a long, passionate smooch.

The next day it happened again. My brain, as usual, assumed that kissing meant he was my boyfriend. He must be in love with me. I asked him about it the next day. He offered a very complicated answer. He told me that he and I were 'kissing friends'. This was my first encounter with that word.

'Are we in love or are we not?'

'Love has nothing to do with this.'

Obviously I must have had the look of dissatisfaction so he continued, 'You are so cute that I love you. But it doesn't mean that we have to be something just because we've kissed. You know,

I have other friends at college who are my sleeping friends'.

'What do you mean? As in sleeping beside you?'

It was not really a silly question. You see, my brain is extremely compartmentalised into neat drawers. In my mind, sleeping next to a boy without sex would also qualify you as a sleeping friend.

Somehow, even though Nicky had given me an insight into the world of sex-for-the-sake-of-sex, this was something different, mainly because I was an involved party here. Here was a guy kissing me every day and having sex with someone else: his 'fuck-buddy', another term I heard for the first time.

Because I wanted to look cool — like, *I see this every day,* and not betray any emotion, I told him that it was perfectly fine with me. He could sleep with as many women as he wanted, because he was never going to get any sex from me unless I was convinced that we were in a committed, monogamous relationship. I added the last bit just to scare him. I knew what men like him wanted. And that was a certain way to slap them, like salami between bread slices, and tighten the grip from the top and the bottom to suffocate them.

But he pursued me for a long time. He told me I was narrow-minded, that my attitude was immature, and that I was being juvenile. Who knows? Maybe some, or even all, of it was true. He could not believe that I had had all these boyfriends, and not had sex with any of them.

'Why won't you have sex?' he said one day.

'I am too young for it, Shiraz Batliwala!'

'Nineteen is old enough. Remember you said your brother had been born by the time your mother was nineteen? Now do that math.'

'That is not a comparable situation.'

'You are not waiting to be married to lose your virginity, are you, like good Indian girls?' he smirked.

'When and to whom I decide to lose my virginity is my business. May I remind you that you are a guy who has new fuck buddies every month? And that, my dear, means that you are not even close to the top of the list of men I would like to have sex with.' Phew!

And so it went on and on and on for a few days. To be honest, with so much sex talk without actual sex, hanging around with each other had also stopped being fun.

Chapter 11

I went back to Bangalore for a long weekend. Nicky came over to see me. It had been a few months since we last met. I learnt he had broken up with Sheeba. Ha, I had known all along it would happen. I told you so, didn't I? I had been expecting it, but I was surprised by how it had happened. In fact, Nicky was totally devastated when I saw him.

'Do you want to talk about it?' I asked him.

'No,' he said. There was silence. After a long pause, he said, 'She is a whore. She is just a bloody slut.'

I was completely taken aback. He was not the kind of guy who used such words for his girlfriends. And he was not screaming. It was a very quiet voice.

There was another pause. 'She called me from Delhi one day, and said she was calling the whole thing off because she was getting married. I missed my exams and went to Delhi. She said that she still loved me, but she had met this guy who was good looking, well settled, and drove a Ferrari. She didn't want to wait. She said life was too short! And men, like the one she was marrying, were few: rich, and willing to marry her right away. He had the money and I didn't.'

'Does he know that you exist?'

'Actually, no. So I went for the wedding.'

'Shut up! Are you joking? Did you really?'

I think it must have been the tone of my voice. We both burst out laughing. 'Yes, she introduced me to him at the wedding, told him I was a friend.'

'How did he seem?'

'Honestly, I don't know — but he had the money, Gauri. Maybe he is a good guy, but I don't know if that is why she married him.'

He was quiet again. I wasn't sure if I should say anything. I let the angels pass — that is what my sister would say. When no one knows what to say, and there is a moment of silence, the angels are passing and everyone should stay quiet. I stayed quiet.

'Two days after she got married, she called up and asked me over to her house. She was half naked in her bedroom. The colour of mehendi on her hands was still red, and she wanted to sleep with me, her ex-boyfriend, whom she had just dumped!'

'You *didn't* sleep with her!' I think if it were physically possible for eyeballs to pop out of their sockets, mine would have.

'You bet I did. And why shouldn't I?'

I thought about marrying for money. I guess some women want rich husbands, and some men want trophy wives, and so, maybe those marriages are perfectly balanced.

'Did you cry over her?' I asked.

'Nah, are you kidding me? Cry, my foot!'

I knew he was lying, but I didn't dispute it. He was an Aries, and they can never be un-cool.

The weekend was over. I had to return to my life in Bombay. Shiraz was waiting for me. He took me out for tea. It was inevitable. When two people want different things from a relationship, it can never work — I mean *never*! So he broke off as nicely he could. I looked on with amusement, quietly admiring his acting skills.

'I am a Parsi and, moreover, I am a Parsi priest. Therefore, I must only marry a Parsi girl. I feel I must set you free, so that you can find this person you are seeking... the one to whom you'll lose your virginity.'

Translation: *Dear Gauri, I have tried to get you to have sex with me, I've done my best, but you remain unconvinced. Therefore, I have no choice but to give up now, since I feel I am wasting my time.*

I saw him in college a few times after that. Every time our eyes met, he would make the saddest face he could. I kept a straight face on the outside, and grinned within.

My destiny brought me face-to-face with Shiraz a few years later one new year's eve. He was at the party with his wife — she was not Parsi.

Chapter 12

I always found it amusing that several people thought that if I had a boyfriend, it meant that I was having sex with him. For most people a relationship was not real without sex. Truth be told, I did not have sex on my mind. I did not even try to evaluate why most people my age were interested in sex and I was not. Maybe all that brainwashing about virgin brides had had some effect on me?

No, it was something else. And it was buried so deep within that I was not willing to confront it.

Then one day I received a letter from my sister, who was now fifteen. She said she wanted to tell me something she couldn't tell anyone. It concerned a close family friend. Instinctively, I knew what it was.

I told Rima I had to go to Bangalore for a few days. I was sitting on my bed, while she worked on one of her assignments on the table.

'What do you think is wrong?'

'Someone is molesting her,' I told her.

'You mean at school?' she asked.

'No, someone I know — someone who is a close friend of our family.'

'How do you know?'

'Because I have been there... more than once.'

This was not an emotional conversation at all.

'How old were you?'

'Once when I was five, and once when I was eight.'

'Someone from the family?'

'It always is, isn't it? Someone your parents would trust.'

'Did you ever tell anyone?'

'I tried telling my sister, but she didn't believe me — she was just a kid. I thought everyone would think I was lying... and this is probably what she wants to tell me because, even though it was many years ago, I think she remembers I once told her about it.'

'You know, Gauru (she always called me that), you are not alone. Half of the girls in this hostel have a story like this to tell. I think it happens everywhere.'

'Somehow I feel that in some way my parents didn't do enough to protect me. They should have been more careful, and done more.'

'Maybe they did the best they could with their experience and knowledge.'

I had carried this resentment in my heart for years. When you are young, you see your parents as perfect. They can never do wrong. It takes a few years to realise that they are just people.

'Do you love your parents?' she asked all of a sudden.

I had never been asked that question before. How can there be an answer to a question that obvious? Yet, I thought for a while before answering.

'I don't know. Maybe I love them because they are my parents, but I am not sure I like them.'

'What do you mean?'

'They are very different people. There is no meeting point between us. I just don't fit into their world. Anyway, I have to go. To see my sister I mean.'

'What will you do?'

'I haven't thought about it yet.'

I said my short and sweet prayer: *God, please help me!*

Child abuse is so common in our society. Every second girl I came across in the hostel had been through it. Yet, most of our families didn't know about it. All of us had cried ourselves to sleep night after night for years together, stripped of our innocence, distrusting the world, and not knowing what to do or whom to tell, feeling shame and guilt, asking why this had happened to us, and not getting any answers. We all came from 'good homes' and 'good families', and therefore we pretended that these things did not exist.

I went to Bangalore for the weekend. My parents didn't know I was coming, and were surprised to see me. The person who had been molesting my sister was a well educated man — a doctor, in fact. As my sister and I talked, my sadness turned into something else.

Now I was angry at him for doing this to my sister, because I knew she would carry the scars all her life. I was angry at my parents for allowing this situation to present itself, and I was angry at the world that this had happened. I was so angry that if I did not believe in non-violence, I would have hurt someone.

I called him up, without any definite plan in my mind. 'I have come home for just a couple of days. Why don't you come and see me?' I said sweetly.

He agreed.

Once upon a time we looked upon him as our foster father. He took us for outings, and had an important place in our lives. When there were things we wanted to tell an adult but couldn't tell our parents, we used to turn to him. We trusted him. Trust — a small word with a big meaning. He had taken advantage of this precious status that we had lovingly bestowed upon him.

He came over with some presents for me.

'Do sit down. Will you have some tea?' I asked.

'Yes, tea will be great.'

We sat down for what he expected would be a casual chat about my life.

'So, how come you are here just for two days all of a sudden?'

'I need to settle some business.'

I called my sister, and parents, to the living room. Only my sister knew what this was about. My parents were surprised to be called into the room.

'Sit down,' I almost ordered them.

No one knew what was going on. Even I didn't know what I was going to do, but God was with me, telling me that I had never done anything so brave, and so right, in my life before. My stomach was churning but, on the outside, my voice was firm and clear.

'You owe an apology to my sister, and I have come here to get it out of you.'

'What are you talking about?'

'Oh, you don't know what I am talking about, is it? Well, I could tell you in front of my parents, but I don't know if you would like that.'

I looked him in the eye. His face turned red.

'Is this what you called me here for?' He was on his feet.

'Did you really think I asked you here for tea?' I glared at him. Words flowed out of my mouth, and I don't know how my brain supplied them to me so quickly. I felt strong and unafraid.

He picked up his car keys and started walking out. My parents were bewildered. By now I was grinding my teeth in anger and controlling every desire to hit him. I clenched my fist, my nails digging into my own flesh, and held my hands together behind my back.

'What's going on?' my mother asked, totally confused.

'He is molesting your teenage daughter under your roof, and you don't even know about it! How could you allow this to happen?'

Big tears were rolling down my hot cheeks, and I could feel my brain bursting out of my skull.

He got into his car. I followed him outside, holding the presents he had brought me.

'You touch my sister one more time, and I will kill you!' I yelled, throwing the presents at the car.

I turned and walked back to the house.

My mother was crying. My sister was crying. And now I was crying too. My father was quietly watching it all. He didn't say anything. Of course it was a shock for everyone.

'I didn't know this was going on. We trusted him. He's been like a family member.'

I knew my mother was sorry at that point, but I was still angry with her. My sister and I have always been the best of friends.

Although I am only four years older than her, she has often said that I have been like a mother to her. But a sister always wants to be just a sister. And, as her sister, I never wanted to play the role of her mother.

My confrontation with this man was a vent for my own pain and anger I had dealt with all alone for more than ten years. It was a symbolic closure. No one can understand the humiliation and guilt that abused children live with, and no child deserves to live with it.

Chapter 13

I returned to the hostel. Being amongst other girls who had suffered like me allowed my wounds to heal slowly. I had never had so many girl friends before I moved to the hostel. I have to say that after being a tomboy for most of my life, it was wonderful to be amongst so many girls.

The sort of things we women discuss in our moments of bonding would make most men raise their eyebrows. We gossip, we bitch, we discuss feelings, we discuss politics, we joke — mostly, we make fun of other people. But even the most sensitive guy would never be able to understand why we constantly ask this one question all the time (and most guys cannot even answer it honestly).

'Rima, how do I look?'

'I'd say above average. Why do you ask?'

'I can't make up my mind whether I like how I look, or not.'

'Why?'

'Well, because my mother always says I have strange features. My forehead is too broad, my eyes and mouth too small, my nose too long, and my cheekbones too high. And I always wanted to get my chipped tooth fixed. What do you think?'

'A big forehead is a sign of intelligence, a long nose means aristocracy, and don't forget that my favourite actress Meryl Streep also has small eyes and high cheekbones. So, all in all you are fine.'

That was why I loved her.

My mother was a very attractive woman, though she was not very tall. She always looked younger than her age. She had been taught, by her mother I guess, to dress up to hold her man's attention at all times so that he would not stray. But I think that also helped her get attention from other men who were not part of the equation.

My father, on the other hand, was fourteen years older than my mother. So, they had more than a generation between them, if we go by what psychologists call a generation gap. Anyway, I noticed that it was easy to spot a good-looking woman, but I didn't see good-looking men like my father too often. He looked every bit a fauji, and he had presence.

Despite his tough looks, he was very soft-spoken. He had never raised a hand on any of us. He had the softest grey eyes that none of the children inherited. And, though I like the clean shaven, boyish look, he had the most dashing moustache that tickled me every time he planted a kiss on my cheeks.

I had all of my father's features, but because of some strange miracle, at a quick glance, I looked exactly like my mother.

However, as I grew older, I became a citizen of the world because nobody could pinpoint my place of origin. I could pass off for an Indian, Egyptian, a Spaniard, a Middle Eastern, and even someone from vague parts of South America.

'You know, Gauru, it's a definite advantage to have looks, but personality matters more. You are not just another brick in the wall,' Rima said, borrowing from Pink Floyd.

Ah... so you are saying that since I don't look that great, I should be thankful that at least I have some personality?

'Thanks, bitch.'

'You have an aura about you.'

I would discover only in the era of the Internet search that my name meant something like that.

'And you have a hot body,' she added as an afterthought to make up for putting her foot in her mouth.

I had straight, brown hair. I was medium built, about five feet five inches tall. Despite all my frequent and failed dieting attempts to look like a person stricken by anorexia, I was not skinny, but luckily I was never referred to as fat either. I was athletic, with good legs — complete with souvenir scars collected at various sports fields. Some of these scars would have the honour of making it to my passport as unique identification marks, but I was always conscious of being top-heavy. It irritated me when boys looked at my bust instead of looking me in the eye when they talked to me.

'I don't have a great body. My boobs are too big,' I responded.

'Guys love big boobs, babes. But, I read in a magazine that women are never happy with their bodies, so you are on the right track.'

'Maybe you do need to be rich to look good like some of the girls in my class. I feel the boys in my college hardly notice me.'

It was a fact. No boy in my college ever gave me a second look. I swear!

'Stop whining. Do you ever look at yourself in the mirror before going to college?'

'Sometimes.'

'What do you see?'

'Myself.'

'Bitch, lemme tell you what I see. I see a girl who wears her sleep-gear to college, who takes three minutes to get ready, who wears the same shorts she made out of an old pair of jeans four years ago, and occasionally there is tooth-paste on her t-shirt… in case you didn't notice. And you wonder why the boys don't look at you?'

Imagine the horror. I had turned out like this after being brought up in a Punjabi household!

'But you also dress like that to college, Rima,' I said.

'Honey, I am studying architecture. We are supposed to have the arty-farty look. And I never have toothpaste on my t-shirt, for the record.'

Chapter 14

I hung around with Rima at JJ College of Architecture so often that some of the students thought I studied there.

I was also reasonably good at art, and used my talent to help my hostel friends complete their assignments in return for favours such as getting my clothes washed, treats at restaurants, etcetera. Sleepless nights went by, colouring perspectives and completing models, listening to Queen and Def Leppard in the background, taking overdoses of coffee. I noticed a strong camaraderie in professional colleges but, at Sydenham, I did not even see all my classmates in the three years I spent there.

In her fourth and final year at college, Rima was elected the General Secretary, and there was a party to celebrate her victory. She put up a show and asked us to help her with it. We decided to reproduce the *Mehbooba* performance from *Sholay*, the biggest Bollywood hit from the '70s.

I was to play the lead singer — yeah, the guy. So much for all the assurances she had given me on my looks! I wore my dungarees, and Rima became Gabbar Singh. Riya and Asha were the dancing girls. We were 'Overnight Stars'. That is somewhat different from saying, 'Overnight, we became stars.' Our stardom lasted only that night. After the show we just hung around accepting the accolades that came our way. This was where I was introduced to Rahul through a someone who knew someone who knew me sort of chain.

A couple of days later, on a Sunday, we went out for lunch to celebrate Rima's twenty-third birthday. Rahul and I were forced to hang around with each other, because we were the only ones in the group who were not a couple. So the juvenile entertainment for everyone else that afternoon was teasing us. He was doing his post graduation in Hotel Management, and I was in my final year.

If I was allowed to extend the term 'mixed breed' to describe breeding of human species, I would have used it on him.

His mother was from Mizoram, and his father was from Uttar Pradesh. She was a Christian, and he a Hindu. Though they had married of their own choice, Rahul had seen a lot of conflict between his parents all through his childhood.

The fights were usually about what religion the children should follow. And, even though all the children had Hindu names, he and his brothers had been baptised.

This is the complicated part of most inter-religion marriages. Love takes a backseat as soon as practical issues surface. Should the children believe in a Hindu, Muslim, or Christian God? If a family member dies, should he be buried, cremated, or fed to the vultures?

Of course, at every opportune moment throughout my life I had been reminded how lucky I was to have been born a Hindu. My parents never disparaged other religions. As children we were taken to churches, gurdwaras, dargahs, and temples. In fact, my father had often told us a dramatic story about a Muslim family rescuing them from the jaws of death during the Partition. Yet there was a sense of superiority — for we were Hindu, and Brahmins at that.

'You have to be born that. It's not something you can acquire or convert to,' my mother would say.

Soon, the jokes our friends made became a reality. Rahul and I started seeing each other. I'm not sure how it happened but it was a bit like keeping a pet. Even though at first you may not have any feelings towards it, you learn to love it. Whatever it may have been from his side, he grew on me like Gypsy, our pet dog, and that is an absolute compliment!

Being in a relationship with him should not have been a problem, but as soon as I became his girlfriend, something about him changed drastically. From being a cool friend, he became a possessive boyfriend. I have no idea why or how that happened. Even my friends who were majoring in Psychology couldn't figure out what made him so obsessive and insecure. But his jealous behaviour drove me crazy.

He had no sisters, and had virtually had no exposure to girls. Worse, I was his first girlfriend. On the other hand, I had had a few boyfriends by now, but not a single one of them had behaved as if he owned me. After a few weeks of romancing and exchanging presents, it became a very stressful relationship. I had lost my sense of freedom, and my mental balance. I had to continuously supply him with information about where I went, who I went with, how long I went for. It was like living in a military camp! Even my parents had never kept tabs on me like that.

But we still hung around together. I can't say now why I didn't end that asthmatic relationship. It was during this relationship that I had my very first migraine. One afternoon I discovered a rock drummer going bang, bang, bang inside my skull. Time went by... we stayed together. He driving me nuts, and I allowing him to drive me nuts.

Soon it would be the end of college — the time to start evaluating what I would do with my life. A few weeks before college ended, I had a dream that felt so real that I could have sworn it really happened.

'Good morning. What makes you so happy first thing in the morning, bitch?' Rima asked. She always woke up earlier than I did, and was already working on one of her assignments.

'Oh, I had this awesome dream...'

'Hmm. Did you dream that you lost your virginity?'

Ignoring her annoying attempts to burst my dream bubble, I carried on, 'I was walking across the football field in my school with a man — a faceless man — and he was pushing a baby's pram. Another little girl in a short dress, with her podgy thighs and pink shoes was holding my hand and walking with me. I owned them — *my* daughters.'

'Hmm. How do you know they were girls? They could have been boys. Did you check their nappies?'

Only Rima had the ability to talk nonsense even that early in the morning.

'No, they were girls. I will only have daughters when the time comes.'

'Aw, come on, what's the difference, Gauru? It's all the same.'

'No, it isn't. Every time I fought with my mother, and asked why my brother could do something I couldn't, the answer was always the same — *because he is a boy.*'

There was a pause.

'You know, a friend of mine from school lost her mother to cancer. Her father allowed her to light her mother's pyre at the funeral, and my parents didn't approve when they heard of it, because according to Hinduism, only if a son lights the pyre of a dead parent can they go to heaven. Is that why people go on having kids until they have a boy, so that they can go to heaven when they die?'

Hinduism is the world's oldest and third most practised religion and maybe the only one not propagated by a single person. I think it's far from weak. Yet, only the boys can have their sacred thread ceremony (Upanayana). Girls are considered impure during menstruation, even ostracised during those days in some homes. Only when a boy gets his head shaved (mundan) is there a celebration. I don't think God ever intended girls to be put on the back burner in his world, but somewhere down the centuries we have been put there.

'I like boys, and I honestly don't think we are superior to them, but I don't think we are inferior either. And just so that I can continue to be the rebel I already am, and because other people would rather not have girls, I hope I have only daughters. In fact, I hope I have four of them because three is a number that sucks!'

Funnily, Rima too was one of three siblings, but she was not just the youngest — she was also the only girl. But the pressure to equal her brothers' status was there. I could always see it. She too came from a modest family. Both her brothers had made it to

IIT (India's premier engineering institute), and then to the US, and they both were extremely successful. Maybe the pressure was self-created, but it was there. She had ambitions of a real career, unlike most of the other girls we were friends with.

'So, are you going for the interview at college today?' she asked, changing the subject.

'I haven't decided. I am not even sure if I should start working or study further.'

'What's the debate?' she asked.

I was glad that there was someone I could discuss these things with.

'I don't want to ask my father for any more money. If I studied further, I would have to continue taking money from him, but if I started working, I could be on my own.'

I had been waiting for the day when I wouldn't have to ask my father for money.

'That's also being very short-sighted! Don't think of only the next two or three years; look at the next ten or fifteen years. Life can be very long at times and, at some point, you may regret not studying further.'

Even today I am impressed with twenty-year-olds who know exactly what they want. I envied all my friends who knew at ten that they wanted to be pilots, doctors, engineers, dancers — and they did all that it took to get there. Even at twenty, I was a 'lost case' wondering why I hadn't studied Economics or maybe Fine Arts.

'Maybe you will get so used to the good life money can buy that you wouldn't want to give it up for an education,' she said.

'And what if I were to die soon, as predicted? My ghost may never leave the earth because I would have so many unfulfilled dreams.'

'Unfulfilled dreams? Like what? Dying a virgin?' she laughed.

I tried not to be put off at her joking about this somewhat serious discussion.

'You know what I really want to do? I want to explore the world. I want to see the Himalayas, go on a safari to Kruger, take a picture in front of the pyramids, walk on the Great Wall. I want to see how the world looks from the top of the Sears Tower; I want to watch a musical at West End; I want to see Mt Fuji... and maybe, when I start drinking, it would be nice to sip a glass of wine in Tuscany with a cute Italian. I want to experience everything in life.

'Maybe I should become a journalist. I already hate accountancy.' That was my major in college.

'You should join the travel industry,' Rima said.

Chapter 15

The thought of the travel industry was attractive of course, because I would see the world, at someone else's expense.

But regardless of whatever I would end up doing, I was as ambitious as Tenzing and Hillary before they climbed the Everest. And, just like them, I didn't have a helicopter to get there either.

Thus began the search for the perfect job. There was no sign of the travel industry waiting for me to arrive, its red carpet rolled out. So I applied to advertising agencies, a research firm, airlines, hotels — wherever I could apply with my qualifications (that I technically didn't have yet in any case).

I was finally going to be a graduate. Thrilling, huh? Far from it. I felt no emotion, neither the excitement of what was going to happen next, nor any feeling of accomplishment. And why would I have those feelings anyway? I was only going to become a part of the statistics — one of the twenty million graduates in India (that number by the way has more than doubled in the last two decades).

There had been something very intense about the transition from protection to independence when I moved to college. But, even though this was the moment when I would be jumping from college to the big bad world, I didn't feel a thing... that is, till I started job hunting. Then there was a flood of emotions.

Leaving school is a reality check. You figure that no one cares if you were the head girl of your school. Leaving college is an even bigger wake-up call, as you realise that no one gives a damn about your Ms. Sydenham '92 title, your athletic achievements, or your struggle for independence. And you realise that you are far from the superstar you thought you were, and that the world, in fact, doesn't revolve around you.

Yes, it doesn't. There are many in the world just like you.

Even though Rima told me that I was not another brick in the wall, I definitely felt like one. I went from interview to interview. More graduates than jobs everywhere. Finally, before my shoe soles wore out, I found a job — as a guest relations executive at a hotel. Ironically, the position was in Bangalore.

Should I take it or leave it?

Of course it was a no-brainer! Rahul was still struggling to get a job. I had turned twenty, and he was two years older.

My brother had no job either. He had completed college a year earlier, and tried his hand at several things, but he could not put his heart into anything he attempted.

I was very thankful because I had that one thing they didn't — a job! I had appeared for many interviews in Bombay too. Many companies were taking too long to respond, so of course I returned to Bangalore and took up the position at the hotel.

College life ended, and I was sad to lose physical proximity to my hostel friends. Everyone went back to their homes, but an invisible thread held Rima, Riya, Asha, and me together. Soon after we returned to our homes, Asha got into some boy trouble, and was not allowed to keep in touch with us for the next few years. A year or so later, Riya got married and migrated to London. Rahul went back to Pune where his parents lived. Hiten and Jigna stayed on in Bombay, and Rima too moved in with her parents in the suburbs of Bombay.

Moving to Bombay had been a death and a rebirth. I had nursed such an obsession for death that it surfaced in my thoughts all the time. And I do remember how it happened. On one of her missions to look into the future (possibly to assess if I would ever be a normal child), my mother had taken me to a palmist when I was around eight or nine. One of the striking lines on my palm is my life line, more so because it is short. I think his assessment was that I would be lucky to live beyond eighteen.

Though his prophecy has been proved wrong — apparent as I write this story as someone who just reluctantly turned forty, it does seem that in some sense what he said was true. I did not realise that this phenomenon would occur again and again in my life. I guess we all die several times, and we are all born again with new thoughts, new visions, and new goals — born as a new person, as the old one dies.

Three years had gone by. I had unlearnt everything I had learnt in the first seventeen years of my life. I was now fiercely independent. No matter how wavering my defiance had been in the past, it now became a dominant trait. I was beyond repair. As I learnt to fend for myself, I was not afraid of standing up for what I believed in, and I didn't mind if the others didn't agree. I recognised what music I liked, and what clothes I liked, what subjects I enjoyed, what food l liked to eat. I even realised that I liked boys who had a cute butt. I was free to make my own choices, and I made them all.

Chapter 16

Reality struck after I returned to my home in Bangalore. My parents were exactly the same as they had been three years ago, but I was unrecognisable in every way. Now I was really a disjointed piece of the family puzzle, more black than brown — the sheep that had at least blended in from time to time.

The only person I could communicate with, without getting into an argument, was my sister, even though we were very different. She was more amicable, accommodating, non-confrontational, sensible, and maybe a little timid. She admired me because she thought I was tough, and because I didn't care about what anyone said or thought, especially if those anyones were my parents! And I admired how she never got into any fights with anyone. She was the apple of my father's eye, and very much the daughter he wanted. But I was not jealous of her anymore, I loved her.

My father had given her and me, two Punjabi girls, authentic south Indian names. She was Nandini. I don't think he ever imagined that our names would have any bearing on the community of spouses we chose. Otherwise, we would have been given names like Sukhbir Kaur and Harbhajan Kaur.

She and I had the same sense of humour. I could start a sentence, and she would complete it. We enjoyed private jokes in public places, because all we needed was to look at each other to know what the other was thinking. Of course, most of these jokes were about the boys our mother was always evaluating for us. Without exception, they were such specimens that they deserved to be joked about.

We knew each other's deepest, darkest secrets, and there was absolutely nothing under the sun that she and I did not talk about — career options, boys, our parents, clothes, politics, ideologies, restaurants, music, movies, and even various fart smells!

Time dragged very slowly as I tried to stay out of trouble. I had already been home for a couple of months now. Rahul and I had been together for over a year. We spoke to each other a couple of times a week.

The phone rang one evening. It was him. He spoke as though he was hypnotised. His exact words to me, without changing a full stop or a comma were, 'I am a believer, and Jesus is the only God I know, and I don't want to go through what I have seen my parents go through. So I am telling you now that if we are to be together, you need to convert to Christianity. Otherwise we can never be together, and I will never speak to you for the rest of my life.'

Yes, exactly. At first I too thought it was a joke.

It was irritating. I was so not prepared for this conversation. I had not combed my hair; I was not even sitting on a chair. And I was next to my mother, who had always despised him. That was the worst bit. My pride was being cut into pieces, and I had to look super cool. I composed myself and tried to signal to my mother that I needed privacy, with some hope that I would get it. Seconds passed. I didn't have the time to think, but it was clear that he was stepping on my personal space, and asking me to do something against my will.

'You know, you breathe down my neck but I have never asked you to change anything about yourself. You do not have the right to ask me to do anything of this sort! You don't own me.'

'Then we will never see each other again. Good bye and Jesus be with you.'

There was a click on the other side and that was the last I heard from him, and of him. A smile spread across my mother's face as I walked off without explaining anything.

When you are past mid-life, and you look back at what it was like to have no job for a few months after college, it seems very trivial. But, when you are just out of college, it is something else! Your friends, neighbours, your mother's gardener, and father's driver have a job. And everyone is always asking you *'What's going on?', 'Did you get that job?', 'Did you hear from that company?', 'What are you planning to do?'*

Rahul had not found a job. His mother had introduced him to the church group to help him cope with his problems.

I don't think they got him a job, but he did dump me as a result.

I always had flexible views on religion, but being asked to follow another religion against my will made me angry.

Maybe education has nothing to do with tolerance, and that is why we continue to divide the world without any justification. Religion is the single largest cause of war. I checked my History book before writing that.

Will our world ever be liberated from discrimination?

Boy versus girl. *Can I help that I was born a girl?*

Hindu versus Christian. *Can I help that I was born a Hindu?*

Rich versus poor. *Can I help that I was born bang in the middle?*

But who cares what I think? Even what Garfield, that lazy cat, thinks is more important than what I think!

A week later the postman left us a note that a huge parcel had arrived for me. It was so big that the poor postman couldn't deliver it on his cycle, so my father drove me to the post office to pick up this big carton that contained everything that was a memory of my relationship with Rahul. When I opened the box I saw the extent of his obsession with me.

Rahul had saved every little napkin I had scribbled on, every little note I had sent him, every little present I had given him, every little pencil I had touched, and even the coasters from restaurants we had gone to together. The only thing he didn't send back was a sweater I had bought him with my first salary.

'What a bum! That was the most expensive thing I bought him,' I said to my sister, 'and it's the only thing I could have used had he returned it.' What was I going to do with used chocolate wrappers anyway?

It was funny and a bit hurtful. He had just thrown me out of his life like a banana peel into the garbage can, and I was cool with it. I felt I could breathe again. My sister and I bought a video of *Robin Hood Prince of Thieves* that weekend, and we rewound at least a hundred times, the scene where Kevin Costner crashes in to save the unwilling bride.

'*Robin, you came back for me*,' she says.

'*I would die for you*,' he replies.

And that is how I got over Rahul, over a weekend.

Chapter 17

Engineering is a four-year course, so Nicky was still in college when I graduated. Now that I was also in Bangalore, we met from time to time. After Sheeba broke up with him, he had gone back to being footloose and fancy free, casual girlfriends followed.

We went out for beer one evening with some of his college friends. One of them was Suraj. Suraj was from Bombay and lived in Nicky's hostel. I told him how much I missed my life there, and he echoed my sentiments. Once a Bombayite, always a Bombayite!

Staying at home after hostel life was like trying to get yourself spoon-fed after you have learnt to eat yourself. And, whatever love my parents and I had for each other during the three years that I was away, vanished like nail paint remover from an open bottle.

The big difference was that living on my own I had found the courage to voice my opinions. I saw no need to hide behind silly pranks. I spoke of things the way I saw them. My parents and I fought about everything: what my sister should study, why my waking up at a certain time interfered with their lifestyle, whether the neighbour's car was olive green or mint green, and even about how I needed to get the shape of the gulab-jamun perfectly round.

My brother still didn't have a job, and I didn't see him trying too hard to get one. Also, my feelings for him were different now. The halo of my admiration for him had disappeared, as I didn't see him as someone superior to me. In my eyes we were equal. And though I was his kid sister and that is something I will always be, at that point I also felt frustrated because he was exceptionally well read and bright, and I felt that he was wasting his life.

I was tough with him — something I had never seen my mother be. One day at the dinner table I asked him, 'So what are you planning to do with your life?' — the famous question Saiff had asked me when I was fifteen.

'It's none of your business.' We both got our fiery temper from our mother whose temper was worse than the two of us put together.

'I don't see you making an effort at all. Are you planning to live off Dad forever?' It was as though I had just poured acid on his open wounds.

'Go to hell! Even if I am doing that, it's not you I am living off!' He flung down his dinner plate, full of food of course; went to his room, and banged the door shut. What a mess — literally and figuratively! My sister got up and started cleaning. Yet, this was only Part I of this Act.

My mother walked up to me, and swung her hand to slap me. I was sure no one my age was still getting slapped by their parents. I held her wrist to stop her and said, 'I am twenty years old. You can't do this to me anymore.'

My heart was beating very fast. This sort of thing was completely unacceptable in our home. Speaking like this was the ultimate blasphemy.

'He is *my* son, and he lives in *my* house, and I am feeding him with *my* money!' she screamed. 'If you have a problem with our living arrangements, you may leave this house!'

'Great. That is exactly what I will do as soon as I can. He is like this because you protect him all the time — because he is your son!'

I don't think my mother ever thought about anything she said. She was even a bit proud that she had this terrible temper. She would say her temper was an inherited 'gift' because she was a direct descendant of Sage Parshuram (a sage from Indian mythology who was known for his ill temper). She had no remorse at the unpleasant words she uttered. She just said things — awful things. As children, all of us were thrashed with anything my mother could lay her hands on. It was partly her temper, and partly her young age... and we can pass the rest of the blame on parenting those days.

I had vivid memories of my eight-year-old brother being whipped with my father's belt. Over the years, I began to despise violence. There are only two ways in which anyone, who has been deeply affected by something like this, will behave. Either he will emulate that behaviour subconsciously, or he will stay away from it consciously. There is no middle ground. And thus I embraced the policy of non-violence. My mother's attitude was always *might is right*. So we all dealt with it — my father, my brother, my sister — and most of the time I did too. And though we were tired of it, no one dared stand up against it.

I locked myself in the bathroom and cried. I was feeling trapped, just like I had felt many times before, in my own home. After I was done with wallowing in self pity, I contemplated two choices: manicure or pedicure. I opted for a shampoo in the end.

I asked God to help me. And of course me being His child, he attended to my application with utmost promptness.

Within days I was presented with a telegram from an airline in Bombay, asking me to appear for the next level of a job interview the following week. It was one of the many interviews I had gone for before returning to Bangalore.

Soon all the fighting was forgotten and I was the star at home again. My parents' love for me came with a tag that read *Conditions Apply*. I had made some unsuccessful attempts as a child to be the things I thought they wanted me to be.

And now, as an adult, I cared much less about impressing them. I could only be myself and not what someone else hoped I would be. Hostel life had done that to me.

And thus, after three months of intermittent fighting at home, I packed my bags and went to Bombay. The day I left my house was the last time I remember ever taking money from my father for survival. And this time I left my home forever. I would only go to my parents' home as a visitor for the rest of my life and any money I have ever accepted from my parents has only been in the form of presents.

I had no idea if I would get the job, but I was determined not to return. The vacancy for this position had been advertised throughout India. Six thousand people had applied for four posts. I stayed at Rima's place till I got the news. I had got the job, and a salary more than five times of what I was earning in Bangalore. One thing was sure. It couldn't be just me; it was God working for me.

My brother finally found his place in the world a few months later when he joined the Indian Armed Forces like my father. He is hardworking, successful, and has an exceptional career at a place meant just for him. Eventually, he married a girl my mother chose for him, and he has two lovely children and a good looking Punjabi wife who is obedient and timid — nothing like my sister or me. And I do love them all.

Chapter 18

I looked around for accommodation in Bombay, and found a lovely working women's hostel. It was well located and, barring some hot men, it had everything a single girl living on her own could want. It was safe, had a pretty decent mess, a fairly large room, a hobby area for those who wanted to read, write, or paint, a public phone, and lots of other girls for company. I settled down quickly and established a routine. A couple of months went by.

One day I woke up with an awful migraine. My senses revolted against any sound, light, smell, and taste. I slept the entire morning and through the night. And the next. I didn't step out of my room; it was as if those two days just didn't happen. Finally, on the third day, I got ready to go to work. One of my hostel mates was surprised to see me.

'There's been communal trouble brewing in the suburbs for the last couple of days. Everyone's staying in.'

'Really?' I had almost been dead to the world for the past two days.

A second later I dismissed her comment. I was sure it was something blown out of proportion by the media. The world loves excuses that help skip work!

I took the train to work. I got off at the station and went to the bus stop. The streets did seem unusually quiet and deserted. No buses were plying on the roads. I tried to get an auto, but I couldn't find one. *Great! The entire world wants a paid holiday, I* thought to myself.

I decided to try the other side of the station. I climbed on the foot-bridge to cross over, and it was only when I was on top of it that I got an idea about the situation. I could see buildings on fire, roads blocked, smoke billowing towards the skies. The horror made me feel sick. What was I going to do? I called my office from a phone booth. Rahman, the office helper, took the call. He told me no one had come to work.

'Go back home, madam.'

'I am at the station. I will take an hour to get to the hostel, but the office is just five minutes away. Can someone pick me up?'

He thought for a few seconds and asked me to wait at the bus stop. 'I will try to arrange something.'

I was sure he would call the cabbie we generally used. Then, I saw him on his scooter. He was not in his uniform and, although his flowing orange beard never bothered me, it somehow became very conspicuous after I became his pillion rider.

'Sorry, madam, the driver refused to take out his taxi. You should not have ventured out today.'

I had put him in that situation, and I was very irritated at my stupidity. Two more of my colleagues landed up at the office, and for the next two nights we ate, slept, cracked jokes and worked with Rahman at the office.

~

I had stayed in touch with Hiten and Jigna. The two were finally going to be married. They had already been seeing each other for five years and, while I had been averaging at least a boyfriend a year, these two had not broken up even once. Unbelievable.

A few days before the wedding, Hiten called up to invite me.

'I will be there,' I told him.

'Are you from the girl's side or the boy's side?' he joked.

'Which side do you want me to represent?'

'Mine.'

'Yeah, and why not? There's always more money-making at

weddings when you are from the boy's side.'

Then suddenly he said, 'I don't know if I can trust you... because you are her friend too.'

'Are you trying to tell me something?'

There was silence for a few seconds. Then he said, 'Are you sure I am doing the right thing marrying her, Gauri?'

Now, how was I supposed to answer that? 'You are asking me this question a few days before the wedding. Shouldn't you have thought about this earlier?'

'I did. I can't put my finger on it. She was the first girl in college I met, and it was just decided that we should get married. Our parents are involved now... it's very complicated.'

Did he know that I had had a similar conversation with her a few years ago?

'It is only as simple or as complicated as you make it, Hiten.'

'You know things have changed. Our roles seem pre-decided and pre-assigned. I must play the husband, and she must play the wife. I feel unhappy that I am marrying someone who doesn't want anything more from life.'

'This is really a conversation you should be having with her.'

'I tried, but she started to cry and said she didn't know what to tell her family. She accused me of wasting five years of her life. She could have married someone else, someone her parents had chosen for her.'

'But are you willing to risk the rest of your life for the sake of these five years? Are you in love with someone else?' I asked him point blank. But honestly, five years was a long time, and if it included teenage years, it was what the Ming Dynasty was to Chinese history — a very long time indeed!

'Wouldn't I have told you if that were the case?'

'So what are you planning to do now?'

'Well, I did call you to invite you to our wedding, didn't I?' he said.

So that was it. He had all these doubts, but he was going to marry her. And he did.

But marriage is much more than just a wedding celebration. Over the years I have realised that even being ninety-nine per cent sure about wanting to marry someone is not good enough. You should marry someone only if you are hundred per cent sure. Every bone in your body, every drop of your blood, must want it. Anything less is not good enough.

And, they married. Despite all those close relationships I had built over the years, this was the only hostel friends' wedding I ever attended. There were fireworks. We all wore our best clothes, and borrowed our mothers' jewellery.

There was a lot of dancing and celebrations, and just like I had predicted, money-making. At every step, we, the friends, demanded money... to allow the groom to get on to the horse-driven carriage, to allow him to get off, to allow the bride to enter her new home, and we even made up our own customs to claim more money.

I love weddings. I like everything about them — the happiness, the fun, the beautiful people, and Indian weddings are the most enjoyable.

Hiten continued to expand his father's business in Bombay, and they lived in a lovely apartment with a view of the sea. Looking back, I realise that we were just out of college, and so young. I wondered what would become of a marriage built upon the foundation of doubt.

Chapter 19

Here I was worrying about other people's lives... little did I know that I myself was going to be in deep trouble very soon — a different kind of trouble though. Even though I had a fancy job, I lost it after three months. Manual ticket stocks were very precious to airlines those days, because if someone laid their hands on them, they could be misused for a lot of money. I was in charge of the office safe that day, and I had diligently checked the contents and noticed one ticket missing. At that point I was too naïve to know the implications of reporting it. The ticket had probably disappeared a few weeks ago, maybe even before I joined.

But I was the one who reported it. And I was given a week's notice to leave. Ironically, the same day, my two other colleagues who had been stranded with me in office on the day of the riots, got a commendation letter from the top management for their fearless commitment to duty. I think it was just their day for handing out letters to the world.

That *life was complicated* would be an understatement. Consider this: when my sister moved to Bombay to study, I had told my parents that I would pay for her since I had this job, and the money. Now I had to pay her college fees, my own hostel fees, bear food expenses, change my wardrobe from a college girl's to a working woman's — to mention only a few of my expenses. Financial responsibilities — and no job.

I called God. *What are you doing, dude?* Though I was quite annoyed with Him, later I understood that He usually supplied me with angels like Saiff and my Math teacher when I needed them. I had gone to one of the best colleges, had great friends, and there was even the magical disappearance of annoying boyfriends. But, from time to time we have to be put through reality checks so that we could learn some lessons in failure, humility, and finally survival.

I thought of my Math teacher that day.

'Life is an individual event, and only you count,' he had said to me. 'Sometimes you win, and sometimes you lose.'

Ironically, failure can be motivating sometimes.

I applied for all possible jobs, even at places that did not have any vacancy. One of them was a hotel that belonged to the Taj Group. I was interviewed by the General Manager for over two hours. He grilled me like a seekh kebab on a skewer. He was concerned that twenty-something-year-olds like me used such jobs as a stepping stone, and didn't stick around long enough to make it worth his while. He was testing me. But necessity is the mother of all lies. I said all the things that he wanted to hear. He gave me the job. I started working.

I had also applied to another airline for a Marketing position that I was very keen on, but hadn't heard from them. And, of course, three days after I joined the hotel, the airline made me an offer. Now, was it my fault that life timed it like this? I was out of the hotel.

This airline job was much better than the one I had lost. Working and having my own money was truly liberating, and every person, man or woman, deserves this freedom. It gave me a degree of control in my life, and the ability to spoil those I loved.

Yet, the meaning of wealth can be quite subjective. To some, it's having a twenty-storey house in New York or owning a private helicopter. For others it can just mean having enough money to pay for three square meals a day.

Maybe it's all about having more than what you had before, yet I realised that I really *needed* only food, shelter, and clothing; everything else was what I *wanted*.

My sister moved to the same hostel I had stayed in when I

was in college. I stayed in touch with my parents. It was a cordial relationship. Soon my brother also left for the Air Force Academy. That's when my parents decided to move to Delhi for good — you know, to be closer to all the Punjabis of the world. So my Bangalore connection was now lost. Rima, my sister, and I met over weekends. Life was good.

I was sent to Delhi for a short training course. One of those days, the city of Bombay was rocked with 13 bomb explosions. Nothing like this had ever happened before. The next day, the city reported one hundred percent attendance.

For a short phase, there were no men in my life.

Nicky's best buddy from engineering college, Suraj, had moved back to Bombay. He lived at exactly the other end of the city. Both of us had lived in hostels and we were full of stories for each other. We chatted on the phone pretty often. He worked with his father, and I was busy as well, so we didn't meet very frequently. He was my spare-date friend. Whenever I wanted a trustworthy escort to a party, meal, or movie, I would make him my date.

One morning my boss called me, and asked me to attend the ITB, a popular German trade fair, in Berlin, on his behalf. I didn't even have a passport. He got it done in two days, and the visa was arranged in less than twenty-four hours.

My mother got the news and called me.

'Listen, child, have a good time, but please don't eat beef,' she said. I already ate non-vegetarian food and somehow that was acceptable.

'But Ma, whether I eat beef or chicken, it is all the same, isn't it?'

'No, it isn't. Chicken is a bird and beef is a cow.'

'I get it, but it's still one dead animal,' I argued.

'Can we agree on something, please? Even if it is stupid to you, it means something to me. Promise me you won't eat beef,' she insisted.

'Whatever...'

Now, that was an excellent word people of my generation used. It was not a 'Yes, I agree,' and it was not a 'No, I don't agree.'

So it was a safe way to end a conversation, and yet do whatever I wanted to do.

My boss gave me a brief on what I was expected to do in Berlin. I was twenty-one, and had never stepped out of India. It was very exciting. As I was leaving his cabin armed with files and instructions, he added, 'It will be cold. Also take formal clothes.'

Sure. It was already March, almost the peak of summer in India. Larry Page and Seergy Brin had not yet founded Google, and researching weather reports was more difficult than finding a nonagenarian in your neighbourhood. Yup, how cold could it be? And so I left with the best clothes I had.

Chapter 20

I wanted to travel around the world. Destiny was helping my dreams come true.

The day for my departure to Berlin arrived. I went to the airport in the evening and... I missed my flight.

Unbelievable, right? Please believe it. I had this fantastic opportunity to travel overseas for the very first time, and I missed my damn flight! Don't ask how it happened, but it was not an isolated incident. As life progressed, I missed more flights than any other person I know, and it was rarely because I reached the airport late. I could write another book altogether on all my missed-flight episodes but, anyway, I had a lot of explaining to do.

Finally, after I had convinced my boss that it was a one-off (that of course we all know is not true), the following day I was on another flight to Berlin.

As soon as I landed on German soil, I got a pretty good idea about what my boss had meant when he said it would be cold. In fact, I understood it better than anyone else because I had landed in Berlin with exactly one sweater and one shawl. It was four degrees that day.

I froze on my way to the hotel. Once there, I headed to the reception where I was supposed to meet Rita Dastur. Rita was my boss's friend, and he had told me that I could turn to her for any help I needed. The hotel gave me a registration card to fill in, and asked me to pay with traveller's cheques. I tried to figure out what to do with them. It was not rocket science, but the form was in German, and English was certainly not the receptionist's first language.

I noticed another Indian standing at the reception. He seemed to be waiting for someone, and had been watching me intently. I could tell that he was an experienced traveller because, unlike me, he was wearing a warm coat. I asked the receptionist to connect me to Rita Dastur's room. Before she could do that, the Indian gentleman turned to me.

'Are you Gauri?'

'Yes, I am.'

'Hi, I am Raymond. I am Rita's friend. She has already left for the day's meetings, but you can come with me.' Rita knew I had missed my earlier flight, and could not meet me as planned, so she had asked Raymond to help me reach the venue.

'Your first visit to Germany?'

'Yes, the first visit overseas, actually.'

'I can tell,' he said with a smile.

He was a very unassuming person, and seemed to be in his late twenties or early thirties. I had no idea who he was, but Rita had asked him to look after me and that was all there was to him.

'It is a huge travel show. I think you should hurry up. Otherwise, you will be lost. This is Germany, and people don't like it if you are late.'

'Give me twenty minutes. I will be with you.' I quickly ran up to my room and dressed as fast as I could. I ran down again as he was waiting for me.

'Where's your coat?' he asked.

'Well, I don't have a coat. I didn't think it would be so cold,' I answered honestly.

'You are going to freeze out there, I hope you know that. It's a bit of a walk,' he said, and then quickly added, 'Wait here. I have an extra cardigan. It's very warm. You can use it now, and return it to me in India.'

'Are you from Bombay?' I asked.

'Yes, I am.'

Only when I met Rita at the India pavilion did I realise that

Raymond and she were friends… and competitors.

Everyone called him Rayo. Rita was impressive. There were hardly any women like her in her generation, but she was a Parsi and that explained a lot. She was definitely older than Raymond, and that also gave me the impression that she was senior to him in corporate ranking. Rayo and I were never formally introduced. I knew his name, and he knew mine.

That evening we were invited to a party hosted by India's Tourism Minister. This was an opportunity for them to showcase Indian culture to the world. So Rayo told me to be ready at seven in the evening so that we could all leave together. At three minutes past seven I got a call. He was screaming. At me!

'This is not India, this is Germany. And here seven means seven, not three minutes past! We all are waiting for you, so make it fast!'

Before I could say anything, he hung up. I rushed down. I was really worried. What if he told my boss?

I was wearing a sari that my parents had gifted me for my eighteenth birthday. It was pure silk — orange, with a green and gold border. I wore the biggest gold and green earnings, and a golden blouse. My boss had told me to take the best clothes, and this was the very best I had. But, as soon as I reached the lobby, my heart skipped a beat.

Everyone was wearing the same business suits they had worn that morning. Rita's was grey. Imagine that: GREY. And they all looked at me in amazement.

Rayo was the first to speak. 'You are late. And why are you dressed like a Christmas tree?' No more and no less.

I could not swallow, and I could not blink.

'Can I go up and change, please? I will take just a minute.'

'No, we are already late. Just get into the car.'

He was annoyed and, I have no doubt, amused.

Rita, he, and I sat in the same car. My face was hot with embarrassment. The tears in my eyes were desperate to start rolling down. Rita came to my rescue. She spoke to Rayo in Gujarati, but I could make out what she was saying. She was telling him to go easy on me since I was just a new kid on the block and he was not. He tried to crack a couple of jokes. I responded with a half-hearted smile.

As soon as we reached the venue, he apologised with a grin, as if to say that it was not his fault but mine to tempt him with my somewhat outrageous outfit. But everything was forgiven from my side. I mean... I did look like one of the dancers invited by the Tourism Department of Government of India to perform on stage. No matter how much I tried to be inconspicuous, I stuck out like a sore thumb.

I stayed with them for the rest of the trip. We worked hard all day, and in the evening we hung around together. I had a great time. They protected me from the big bad wolves (there were several at such events). I took advantage of their niceness, asking to be taken to every club, bar, and restaurant that was worth visiting — all in Rayo's warm cardigan.

On one of our outings together I dug my strong teeth into a beef burger. It was yummy. Would I have done it had my mother not forbidden it? I don't know.

I headed back to Bombay with a present for Suraj — two tapes of Jethro Tull, his favourite band. Rayo returned a few days later. He had told me I could return his cardigan at his office. I knew where it was. Everyone knew where it was. It was one of the biggest travel companies in the country.

So a week after I had returned, after dry-cleaning the cardigan, I went to his office and asked for him. I was suddenly being treated like a VIP. I was still a little confused. I was escorted to his cabin. It was only then that I realised that he was the owner of the company.

Oh my God!

I was suddenly conscious of his corporate position. A little fazed, my mind reeled back to Germany. I tried to remember if I had said or done anything inappropriate. I had been treating him as if he were some school chum, slapping him on his back and muttering occasional obscenities. Of course he had known all along that I did not have a clue who he was. Now he sat watching my bewildered face with utmost enjoyment, aware that I was completely confused about how I should behave with him now.

'Thanks for the cardigan,' I said returning his sweater to him, tongue-tied, and suddenly on my best behaviour.

'You are welcome. You have stretched it, especially at the chest,' he smiled.

And right then I knew that nothing had changed between us. 'Shut up,' I said. 'You are the man on top. I didn't know that. How old are you?'

'How old do you think I am, darling?'

He called everyone 'darling'... even his wife. He said that he met so many attractive women that it was easier for him to just 'darling' everyone than put his foot in his mouth and call someone by the wrong name. I understood that. I call people by the wrong names (almost always).

'I don't know.'

He was, in fact, just a bit younger than my mother. In a way, if I had known who he was when we met in Berlin, we would have never become the great friends that we became. After that first trip to Germany, Rayo and I were together on several business trips together. I changed jobs, but we were both in the same industry and our paths crossed frequently. He was one of the most straightforward people I have ever met. I can say he became my mentor. He encouraged me whenever my chips were down, and he was by my side for every big career decision I took. I always relied on him for those things.

He said whatever he wanted to say in simple words, and no sugar coating. Take it or leave it. I liked that.

He was a tycoon in the industry. Yet, he was modest, and I truly admired his humility. His wife and I also became friends, and I was warmly welcomed to their home.

He would sit beside me at fancy official dinners, and with a sweet smile that never betrayed what we were talking about, tell me that my nail paint was chipped. Chipped nail polish was bad grooming, he'd say. He wanted me to be perfect. I learnt so many things from him for free that no B-school could teach you even if you paid them a lot of money!

His travel company was an inheritance. It had been set up a couple of generations ago. It was one of the first few travel companies in the country. His father and his uncle were pioneers in the travel industry, and they had created a legacy that he was destined to take forward. It was understood, even when he was very young, that this would be his future. He would have to take charge one day and run the empire.

'How did it feel to have always known what you were going to do?' I asked him one day.

'I never paid any attention to it, darling. I was brought into the business as a teenager, and this is the only thing I have ever known or done.'

'Doesn't it bore you?'

'It doesn't bore me, but there are many other things I would still like to do. Someday, I may have the chance to do them.'

In some strange way, his legacy was also his trap. He had everything, but no freedom to do the things he wanted to do. There was no time to smell the roses, as they say.

We talked about serious things, but honestly, more often we talked about mindless things. And we laughed a lot. I always wondered why he was friends with someone like me, a kid and a nobody in the trade. The answer to that came to me several years later, when one day his wife called me up and asked me over for lunch.

'I would love to. Are you celebrating something?' I asked her.

'No. In fact Rayo is not well, and his spirits are very low. I think he needs some fun, and you are the only person who can brighten him up.'

Bright. The word my name signified.

Chapter 21

And that was how — working, travelling, losing jobs, finding jobs, and partying a bit with my sister — I spent the year after returning to Bombay.

Jigna and Hiten were the first amongst all my friends to have a child: a bonny boy. He was born just a year after they were married. I went to see the baby the very day he arrived. They had many visitors, and their life seemed perfect. I stayed for a long time, until everyone else had left. Hiten was not in the room when I cheerfully asked her, 'So how do you feel, Jigna, being a mommy now?'

'Have you noticed how weird Hiten has become?' Her answer wasn't related to my question at all. 'His behavior is so strange. I don't know what he does all day. He is never home. I don't seem to be his wife, but his maid.'

She had just become the mother of an amazing baby boy. It was supposed to be one of the happiest days of her life.

'Why don't you do something with your life?' I said. 'Maybe go out and work? Help with his business? It will help you get out and develop some interest outside the house too.'

'I have a baby now... I have responsibilities.'

'Come on. The world is full of working women, who also have children.'

'It's too late now.'

I couldn't believe my ears. Too late? She was just twenty-two.

'Maybe some mental stimulation would help your relationship.'

'Maybe. I could become a teacher when the baby is old enough to go to school.'

'That's a good idea.'

The baby started crying. Though I felt her pain, I was not interested in being a part of this conversation.

They were both my friends. I couldn't tell her what I already knew, and I couldn't tell him what she had confided to me.

Besides, I was the fun gal. I was the one they hung out with because they wanted to paint the town red. Now, why did I have to deal with their problems?

I did not deliberately start spending lesser time with them, but I got very busy at work. My work took me to many places, and with all the travelling, it was difficult to manage my time.

Suraj and I met from time to time. One day, quite suddenly, it struck me that he was good-looking. I found myself ogling at him, and so did he (I mean notice me ogling at him). He was tall, a pleasant change after all my short boyfriends, and the hours spent in the gym made his body worthy of a second look. He had beautiful brown twinkling eyes, and a cleft chin that looked very nibble-able. I think he almost caught me with that thought. And the way I looked away, embarrassed, was a sure sign of the naughtiness running through my mind. Worse, we went out to a party one evening and I saw him talking to a good looking girl. I felt annoyed just looking at the two of them together. I developed an instant dislike towards her, and it was very obvious.

Nicky had graduated and found work in Delhi. My parents were in Delhi, and thus, we were able to meet each other often enough. He was working with one of the largest manufacturers of tractors, and his first assignment was selling these in north India. Given the fact that no one in the cities drove tractors, he was often going to villages trying to sell them to farmers, who spoke no English. Nicky saw his job as a punishment. It was comical. I could barely imagine him, this cool dude, style guru, Paris-returned, speaking in Haryanavi, not even Hindi, with dealers, trying to explain why they should buy his tractors.

'Tell me, how is it that I slog my butt off studying engineering for four freaking years, and I'm out selling tractors in villages that have no electricity and water... whereas you, who scored less than me in Math in school, and have a degree that cost you only three years of your life, have this glamorous job that allows you to globetrot? Life is so unfair!'

'School scores are always inversely proportionate to success in working life,' I laughed. 'It would be really unfair if you continued to do well all the time!'

These days the love of his life was Tara. I had never met her, but I think he had already been seeing her for over a year when we had this conversation during one of my trips to Delhi.

'I need to go somewhere this evening. Come with me,' he had said over the phone one evening.

'Sure. What should I wear?'

'Something nice.' That was all he said and hung up.

My father dropped me at Ranbir's place. Ranbir had been our friend since school. Nicky came over to pick me up. As soon as I saw him, I started to tease him about Tara. He smirked. Maybe Ranbir didn't know about Tara, and that's why Nicky didn't want to talk about her. Boys have all these silly rules. We got into the car, and before I could ask about anything, he said, 'We are going to a wedding.'

'A wedding? Whose wedding? You and I don't know anyone who is getting married, and we don't even have a present. *And* what I am wearing is not something I can wear to a wedding!' I muttered all my girl problems.

'We are going to Tara's wedding.'

I looked at his face. Was he joking, or was he serious?

He was serious.

'When did this happen?'

'Last week. Her parents fixed it. He has to go back to London next week, and that's why it happened so suddenly. I don't want to go to her wedding alone. She'll think I am heartbroken.'

I narrowed my eyes and stared at him.

'Don't take me,' I told him, 'because I might want to slap her. How can she marry someone else if she loves you?'

'You don't understand, sweets. I am not a match. I can't afford this fancy wedding at this glitzy hotel. And she's migrating to London. Have you seen cattle? They can be let out to graze in the grass, but eventually they are tied to a post at home. I was lucky to have had the chance to love her.'

'What do you mean? If she really loved you, she could have come away with you. How could her family force her to marry someone she doesn't love?'

'She is not being forced, she has accepted it. There is a difference.'

I noticed Nicky was no longer the brash teenager angry at the world for getting jilted. He understood the ways of the world now. He was telling me that love and marriage didn't always have to be connected. And here I had been thinking about what anything else had to do with it!

The wedding was gorgeous, and so was Tara. I felt like kicking Nicky for bringing me to a wedding without giving me the opportunity to dress for it. I stuck to him, and several times during the evening, I found myself asking him the same question: 'Are you okay?'

'You sound worse than my mother when you ask me that.'

We stayed at the wedding forever. Drinks were flowing, and Nicky drowned his sorrows in them. Only occasionally I reminded him that I didn't drive — it was just one of those things I never learnt to do. The original plan was that he would drop me at my parents'. But they lived very far away and he was too drunk to drive me back. And, in a city like Delhi, taking a cab at that hour was out of question.

But hey, this was just Nicky. He lived close by, and he suggested that I stay over at his place. I didn't have any clothes for the night, but that was hardly a reason for me to hang around with Tara till daybreak! So I agreed.

Nicky lived with his grandmother. He suggested that he and I sleep in his room, since his grandmother would wake up early and sing bhajans, and it might not be appropriate for her to see me in the living room wearing his shorts and t-shirt (yes, that's what I wore to bed that night), or see him suffering from a hangover first thing in the morning when she was trying to connect with God.

So, for the first time ever we were in that situation — same room and same bed, and not even twin beds. He offered to sleep on the floor.

'Don't be stupid. Sleep on the bed with me,' I told him.

This was real life, not *When Harry Met Sally* where we would end up having sex, and eventually find out that we were in love.

We both lay down. I hadn't yet fallen asleep, I could hear his breathing getting heavier. It was dark, but I could see him. I was sad for him. How could this happen twice in a lifetime? For the umpteenth time that evening I asked him,

'Are you okay?'

He didn't reply. He was crying.

I put my arm around him and said, 'It is okay to cry, Nicky.'

We were facing each other on the bed, and he was so close to me that I could smell the alcohol in his breath. We were not buddies at that point. Maybe he was even comfortable crying because I was a girl. He cried, and cried, and cried. He only had one thing to say again and again, 'Why the fuck does this happen to me?'

I wish someone ran a class where you were taught the answers to questions like that!

Chapter 22

I returned to Bombay, and the clock kept ticking. One afternoon, Suraj called up my office to ask if I was free for a movie. My colleagues told him I hadn't shown up at work. He called up the hostel. I came to the phone not aware of who had called me. I was running a fever. Even though I lived far from his place, he decided to come down to my hostel to take me to a doctor. And he paid the doctor's fee. Now that is a dead giveaway in the game of flirting. The next day, after work, he came back to check on me.

The mutual attraction was undeniable and intense, but neither of us would say anything. How we women wish that all relationships could stay in this zone forever, but it's like sitting under a sky full of twinkling stars, hoping that the night never ends!

Suraj introduced me to Suresh and Ajay, his childhood buddies, and we started hanging around together. By then he and I were flirting in front of two other guys — yes, one happy family. One day he got tickets for a live Bon Jovi concert.

Now, not only did I find Bon Jovi delicious, but with his celebrity- and my non-entity status in this world, I could drool at him for hours without anyone thinking I was desperate. No one thinks ogling at unattainable sex symbols is un-cool!

And Suraj had got us tickets to see this super sexy man in flesh and blood. So we went to the concert. There was only a small problem — there were exactly ten thousand people in front of me.

'I can't see anything,' I said to Suraj.

'You can sit on my shoulders if you like,' he said.

'You are joking.'

'No, I am not. I want you to have fun.'

Ajay and Suresh helped me to get on his shoulders, and I watched almost the entire concert sitting on them, just like girlfriends do. When I got down, he was holding me. That was when Bon Jovi sang *This ain't a Love Song*.

Nothing was said or explained. We were just kissing — in public, in the middle of a crowded concert with over twenty thousand people.

Suraj's father was a first generation entrepreneur. He had built enough for Suraj to take forward — a business empire, at least a small empire. For Suraj, his work came first, and though I loved my job, he was my priority. I left my comfortable surroundings, and rented a tiny one-room apartment closer to his home, so that we could have more than just a weekend relationship. Ironically, now that I was closer, and no longer had my hostel friends, I found myself spending even more time hanging around waiting for him.

Sometimes he would come with Ajay and Suresh, and we would go out for ice-cream. He would play video games, while I chatted with Ajay. No new girlfriend wants to spend time with her boyfriend's best friend, while he is trying to get the top score in a stupid video game, but that's what you get when you have a boyfriend your age.

Yet, there had never been a time in my life when I had been so madly in love. My heart glowed like a thousand-watt bulb. I could hear music when none was playing. I could see rainbows when the sky was grey. I could smell him even when he was not around, and somehow, the pupils in my eyes had become heart-shaped. That made me look very dumb, but love has that effect on some people.

I loved him and everything about him quite crazily. Suraj had everything I dreamt of in a guy. Neither was he idiotically possessive, nor was he trying to change my religion, and he was definitely not trying to convince me to have sex with him. He was my first true love, and there is something so special about being in that place that, no matter what follows in your life, that place is irreplaceable. A few days before I turned twenty-three, we lost our virginity to each other.

When we made love that day, every inch of me — body, spirit, heart, and mind wanted it.

I met his family. And, one day, he proposed to me. It was a very I-think-we-should-get-married sort of a proposal. By then I was literally living in his house anyway.

His parents were very different from mine. As their only son, he wanted to look after his parents, as most sons in India do. His parents were nice, and they tried their best to make me feel at home. Having their son's girlfriend over was also a new experience for them, but they tried to show me how they lived. They encouraged me to speak in Konkani so that I could speak to everyone else in the family. I went to all their family dos, and was introduced as their future daughter-in-law. Soon I started doing all that was expected of me. I dressed like they wanted me to, I ate what they ate, and I even spoke how they wanted me to. Yet, there were times when I was at a loss when asked to wear or do something.

Now here is a fact that you already know: I can be slotted into the category of people who, firstly, don't like to be told what to do and, secondly, if told to do something, will usually like to do the exact opposite. If I am asked to take a right turn, my instinct will tell me to go left. This was a manufacturing defect. So following 'suggestions' from my to-be-in-laws was not easy.

'Why can't I wear a skirt at home?' I asked one day.

'In our family, they think it is disrespectful to show legs.'

'But that is how I have always dressed.'

'You can wear what you like, just don't do it in front of them.'

'That's hypocrisy.'

But I tried to 'adjust'. Suraj did not necessarily agree with them, but he didn't want to be the one to bridge the gap. He turned a blind eye to these situations. I don't think his parents appreciated my choice of career either. They were open to a girl with a career — his mother was a doctor after all, but they were concerned that I was made to travel too much.

'But this is what I do for a living, and I love it.'

'Yes, but when you have to raise children you will find it very difficult to balance your life with a job like this.'

'Let's see. Maybe I could study further, and change my line of work.'

I was even planning to change my career so that it could suit his lifestyle. But I did want to go back to college for post graduation.

'I am thinking of a Master's in Marketing.'

'How will you manage it?'

'I will do a three-year evening programme. That way I won't have to give up my work. And I will also have enough money to pay for college.'

'Money is not a problem.'

Money was never a problem for him. His father had worked hard to build what he had, but Suraj had always had enough money. If his car was smashed, he would be given enough to get it fixed. If his bike was stolen, his dad replaced it. And I knew that if I married him, I would never have to worry about money for the rest of my life. I would not have to work — at least not for money.

But why would I want to give up my financial independence, lock myself up in a golden cage and hand over the keys to someone else?

I went back to university and registered for a three-year evening MBA programme. Suraj paid my first term fees because he didn't see any difference between his money and mine.

There was never any doubt that we loved each other, but with time, we began to fight. Suraj was not short-tempered, but he was always willing to get drawn into a debate. And he liked to win. So did I. Thus, we would be at loggerheads pretty often.

I accused him of not giving me enough importance, preferring a video game to spending time with me, of not appreciating my efforts to blend with his family, and once we even fought because he gave me a stuffed toy for my birthday! Imagine! A stuffed toy! Who wants *that* from a boyfriend! All in all it was a pretty passionate relationship. We fought passionately, and we made up passionately.

Chapter 23

During one of those days, out of the blue, my phone rang at six in the morning. I answered it, half asleep. Jigna was sobbing at the other end.

'Gaaaurrrri…,' she couldn't get any another word out of her mouth.

Though I had stayed in touch with her, she had never said anything specific about the issues between husband and wife after that day at the hospital, and I definitely didn't want to be the one to bring them up.

'What's up?'

There was no reply.

'Are you okay? Is Hiten okay? Is the baby okay?'

The baby was about to turn one in a few days.

'Gauri,' she sobbed, 'he... he has another girlfriend.'

There was silence.

'You want me to come over and talk to him?' I just said whatever came to me. That early in the morning, my brain was not even processing the information quickly enough.

'No. I don't know what to do. I am having another baby. Tell me what I should do.'

'Oh God! You should leave him.'

'Where would I go? I can't go back to my parents. They will be shattered to know that my marriage has not worked out. They will lose the respect of their friends. And, what about money to raise the kids? What am I going to do?' she howled.

'I told you to get a job. If you had one, you may not have been in this situation. How could you not see this coming? And why are you having another baby amidst all this?' I was getting impatient with her.

'Gauri… I don't know what to do now.'

'Okay, give me some time. I will come over.' I was wide awake now in any case.

'No, please don't. He will know I have been talking to you.'

'So what? Everyone needs someone to talk to.'

'No, I don't want you to come here.'

'Okay, I won't. But listen, I live alone. If the situation gets out of hand, come here, all right?'

That was just about the best offer I could make in those circumstances.

She could not stop crying. I felt sorry for her. I just stayed on the line — neither of us saying anything, she sobbing and I listening to her sob. Marrying your first love is almost always a big mistake. They were just teenagers when they met each other. Even in my early twenties, I was still learning about myself. I could not understand how they had sustained their relationship for so many years. He had been working, and all the exposure, reading, debating had changed him into a person who wanted more in his relationship. It did not justify what he was doing, but it was inevitable.

I thought many times about why she had called me of all the people she knew. Maybe it was because I was living on my own. Or maybe because she really had no one else to call. Some orthodox family systems discourage discussing feelings in a relationship. When you are married, there is no reason for it not to work out, no scope for sadness. So, what's there to discuss? Especially, if you have chosen your own spouse. You better be ready to accept the consequences. Thousands of marriages survive like that.

She and I spoke several times after that. It was always the same thing. He was now bolder about his extramarital relationships. The first time she had confronted him, there was some remorse. He was sorry, and he had seen her as the victim. But, as time passed, his old ways resurfaced. That she had chosen to forgive him and ignore his actions didn't make him love her. And now the remorse had gone too. But she didn't leave him.

One day, some months later, Suraj and I went to a party where I bumped into Hiten. He was alone. I did not tell him what I knew, but when he and I had a few minutes alone, I asked him how Jigna was.

'Do you remember that discussion I had with you just before we were married?' he said.

'Yeah.'

'It was the biggest mistake of my life. I should have never married her. I knew we were not right for each other, but I kept trying to convince myself it would be okay. I had become such a different person by the time I finished college, and she was still the same girl I had met when I was fifteen. She is still the same girl. It isn't okay... it will never be. I don't love her, and I cannot tell you the things I am doing to her.'

I didn't tell him I already knew.

'Is this how you are going to live the rest of your life?'

'What else can I do? She can't even get a loaf of bread by herself, and we are raising two kids together.'

'Why did you have kids in this situation?'

'She felt having kids would change things — make me love her! But it didn't change anything.'

'It will be very bad for the kids to see you both like this.'

'It may be worse if we leave each other.'

I have never understood how suffering an unhappy relationship is acceptable to people. Or how they convince themselves that it is fair to raise children in that environment. But no day is like any other, no people are alike, and no lesson the same.

Chapter 24

Suraj and I fixed a date for our engagement. I walked a tight rope balancing my work, college, his home, and my home. We would make plans to meet, along with Suresh and Ajay. He would often call up and say he couldn't make it. He usually offered reasons like – *too tired, too late, can't get out, have things to do* and, at times, even *no mood.*

Still, there was nothing I wanted more in my life than to be with him, and I would've fought the whole world for it if I had to. But it was not the world but Suraj himself I ended up fighting with. I had been making all the effort to do things right, and soon I started feeling stretched — like a rubber band. And a rubber band can be stretched only so much before it snaps.

It was yet another rainy day. Ajay and I were sitting in the balcony at my home, watching the rain pitter-patter, waiting for Suraj.

'What are you thinking about so seriously?' he asked me.

'About Suraj and myself.'

'I know what you are thinking,' he said. 'Don't blame him. Ask yourself why it is like this.'

'Why do you think it is like this, Ajay?'

'Because you don't meet him halfway. You take eight steps, and he takes two.'

'Is that what you see?'

'A blind man can see that, Gauri. You have no one but yourself to blame.'

He was right. I could not recognise myself any more. The problem was that I had not yet learnt to love myself. I didn't value myself to believe that I deserved to be loved as much. I had allowed myself to be lost in this relationship. I knew only about giving and not taking what I rightfully deserved.

The engagement ceremony was the following week. I started to have all these doubts because I was trying too hard and, sometimes, when you have to do that, it just doesn't seem worth it. I became quieter, and spent a lot of time thinking. Suraj sensed it. He knew there was something wrong, but didn't know what it was.

We went out for a walk on the beach. I sat down next to him, and told him what was going on in my mind. He listened very quietly.

'What do you want to do?' he asked.

'I don't know, but I don't think getting engaged is a good idea right now. I just want some time to think about it. I cannot spend my entire life trying to be someone I am not. I need some time to clear the cobwebs.'

'You are leaving me, aren't you?'

'No, I am not. I just want some time to think.'

'You want to think? You are not a person who thinks, Gauri. You are a person who feels. When an emotional person like you starts thinking, I know exactly what happens next.'

'Look, this is not easy for me. I love you, but I am not happy. Why am I not happy if I am with the person I love?' I didn't think this was going to be easy.

'So be it. I can't force you to be with me anyway. But I will do my best now that I know how you feel.'

Maybe I should have told him this earlier. I had made a mistake by allowing him to take me for granted, and he had made the mistake of doing it. He did not think I would ever have the courage to retaliate.

My parents had no idea what was going on. They arrived on schedule for my engagement, and I had to tell them, three days before my engagement, that I was taking a break from the relationship. I thought they would be mad at me for having made them come down all the way, but one thing I have learnt from life is that parents are always unpredictable.

'You have saved yourself from a lot of pain,' they said.

Maybe they understood what I was going through.

'We will find you a nice Punjabi boy. Someone has told us about this boy living in Canada—'

Ah, now how did I not see that coming? Of course they didn't mind! One broken engagement was only a sign of hope that I might end up marrying a Punjabi boy of their choice.

The situation between Suraj and me worsened. The more I wanted to be alone, the harder he tried to prove that he loved me. It was very bad timing. He promised me we would never fight again. He said he would change everything about himself I criticised. He apologised for all the times he had not been there for me. And all his desperate efforts had exactly the opposite effect on me, because I was just not getting any space. He would call me several times a day, and come to see me every day even when I didn't want to see him. We were two people madly in love, but so wrong for each other! Our fights were usually so intense that we always ended up hurting each other.

'How is he doing, Ajay? Take care of him.'

'He is pretty bad. Is there any way you can make this work?'

'I am trying, but I feel claustrophobic. I just want some time out,' I said candidly.

'How do you expect a guy to cope with it, Gauri? First you are there all the time, and now you are beating a retreat so quickly that he has no time to adjust.'

'Would I have to live all my life like this? Every time I want him to take me seriously, would I have to threaten him I might leave?'

'Well, he is trying.'

'Maybe it is too late.'

I was confused, and this was not helping me at all. Nicky called me from Delhi. He was unhappy with both of us. Suraj and he had that unbreakable engineering college-hostel-buddies bond between them. Yet, he could take no sides, and he didn't want either of us to be miserable.

Our engagement had been postponed indefinitely. Of course, his parents also knew that we were having trouble, but there was no interference from anyone. Then, one of those days Ajay called me up at office.

Suraj had locked himself in his bedroom and consumed poison. I was shocked. Luckily, Ajay had found him in good time, and he had got him to a hospital quickly enough.

I didn't know what to do. I appeared calm, but I was also very angry. How could he do something so... insane? I wondered if I should call him or visit him. In the end I did neither. I called his sister. She was furious with me because they could have lost him forever — because of me!

'I am not worth it,' I cried over the phone.

'You bet you are not,' she said, adding that she did not want me anywhere near her brother. The relationship with his family was now irreparably damaged.

I called his father.

'I am genuinely sorry for what has happened,' I sobbed.

'It is okay, Gauri. It's not your fault. We will look after him. And, as for the two of you, let me tell you as someone much older than both of you, I know you love each other but I think you are terribly wrong for each other. This is not a relationship that would give either of you any happiness in the long run. You should just move on.'

This was the father of the boy who had almost died because of me. And he was telling me the truth. Sometimes, it is so useful to have the wisdom that comes with age. You can see some things that younger people can't, especially if they are 'blind' in love... crazy love.

Chapter 25

Depending on the circumstances, having an elephant's memory can be a blessing or a curse. It was as if every moment I had spent with Suraj had been videotaped in my brain. For the next few days it automatically replayed everything all the time. Strangely, it replayed only the good things. I had to keep explaining to myself why I had taken the stand I had. I reported sick at work for the next few days. I was not really ill, but felt I was. I flipped through our photo albums every hour. I didn't call my sister or any of my friends. Ajay came to see me one day. I wanted to know how Suraj was. Ajay was honest. But listening to him made me feel worse, and so, I stopped meeting him.

There was a pattern. Thinking-crying-thinking-crying and so on. I hadn't thought about all the practical issues that played a part in making relationships work. I had always assumed love was enough. It was a painful reality. Most of all I had to live with the fact that this relationship had ended without either of us really ending it.

I returned to work only to learn that the airline I worked for had been losing money. It was put up for sale, and I decided to move on before it was sold. I had more responsibilities than anyone else my age I knew. I got the opportunity to work on a short-term project with a company that was organising a Sotheby's auction.

Zaid and I shared the cabin at my new workplace. We had the

singles-at-work-syndrome: no kids to send to school, no families to say goodbye to, and no one to insist we eat our breakfast before we left for work. And therefore we both usually arrived a little earlier than the rest of the office.

First thing in the morning he would get a couple of calls, and he would speak under his breath in monosyllables.

'Is that your girlfriend who calls you every morning?' I asked once.

'I don't have a girlfriend. Not at this point, I mean.'

'Oh, okay. The way you mutter under your breath, it seems you are exchanging sweet-nuthins.'

'Far from it.'

He didn't explain. And, how could he? It was the other boys at office who would call him every morning to find out the fitting of my shirt — to check if a visit to his cabin was worth the trip that day or not.

During the course of this project, I was stuck with an awful boss — a good-looking young woman who suffered from permanent PMS. She believed she was the only one smart enough for the fun jobs. So after all the responsibilities I had handled globetrotting, and doing things that made a difference, I was asked to send the post, follow it up and see if clients had received it, and of course fix her appointments because her fingers were too precious to be wasted on dialing phone numbers.

Zaid could see how she was driving me crazy. All we did during our lunch breaks together was bitch about her. I was glad to have him around. Soon I wasn't just taking advice from him about handling my pain-in-the-butt boss but also about life, Suraj, and my sister's college, etcetera.

He told me he had never met someone so young, who had such control over her life.

'Why do you always make your life more difficult than it has to be?' he said once.

'What do you mean?'

'You left your home when you could have stayed, you spent all your money on your sister, even though you could've saved it, you chose to not marry someone, even though you could have had a comfortable life,' he paused, 'and you fight with everyone to get your work done!'

'I get paid for getting the job done,' I laughed.

Zaid had two deep dimples, and a bright smile. He hailed all the way from Assam. He was brainy and well-read, and had a great sense of humour. He was always full of stories — Greek mythology, political tales (and made the subject quite interesting), and stories of his childhood.

The state of Assam had been witness to unprecedented violence when he was in high school. He had been sent away to Delhi so that his education would not suffer. Some of his school friends had joined the army, some had become militants fighting for the cause, and some had even died. Before moving to Bombay he had lived in a co-ed hostel — sharing a room with two girls from his class. His family still lived in Assam, but his eldest sister lived in New York. And, he was the youngest of four siblings, an even number!

It was just a few days since things with Suraj had taken a turn for the worse. I hated living alone, and everything in my house reminded me of Suraj. My heart hadn't healed, and I desperately needed to move to another place. Zaid too was looking for a place, so we decided to rent one together. I had no designs on him.

We moved into an apartment with two rooms any flatmates would choose. We had a rent kitty, a house-running kitty, and a food kitty. All expenses were shared. My sister and he got along very well too — both were Bob Dylan fans.

This was when nineteen-year-old Lakshmi came to work for us. She was smart despite a lack of education. She was also loyal, efficient, and had integrity. With the right ingredients, she could have taken charge of her life. With the right education, her life could have been very different. I liked her.

In the meantime, my boss kept making me feel like a brainless robot, and though everyone in the management knew how I felt, there were no options available. Three months later I switched jobs. And where do you think I went?

To the Taj group of hotels.

Yes, an impossible co-incidence in the maze of life where

the past is intertwined with the future at every stage. This time I joined a different department. The person who had interviewed me a few years ago had gone higher up the ladder, and was my new boss's boss. I spent an entire year trying to hide from him. It was pretty much like playing Tom & Jerry. Finally, one day, we were face-to-face. Everything started to happen in slow motion, and every second was a minute long. He searched my face, trying to place me. I looked at him innocently, as if I had never seen him in my life before. How could he forget a girl who had spent two hours trying to convince him she was going to work at his hotel till she retired, only to leave three days after joining?

I was sure I was going to get the boot. Unbelievably, I didn't.

One evening, Zaid and I had just seen my sister off at the hostel, and were walking towards the cab when he got stung by a big, black bee. His hand instantly swelled up. I offered some sympathetic oohs and aahs.

'Actually, I was carrying it around in my pocket, and got it to sting me so that I could get some attention from you,' he smiled.

I recognised it immediately — of course he was flirting.

That evening we had planned to eat out because there was nothing to eat at home. It started raining. There was not a cab in sight, and we were soaking wet.

The first rains give you a high, have you noticed that? Not when you are trying to head home with five children and extra shopping bags... but when you are out with a man alone, oh yes, it facilitates the rush of adrenalin that can dangerously lead to other things.

Cold and shivering, we walked a long way before we could find a restaurant that would entertain soaking wet customers. And when we did find one, the first thing we ordered was vodka. Rain and drinks make a perfect recipe for disaster. By the time we reached home that night, our situation had changed completely and suddenly. He had moved into my bedroom, and his room was now our living room where we entertained visitors.

In hindsight, I had walked right out of Suraj's life and into Zaid's arms without thinking. All said and done, that's one of the fastest, the stupidest, and maybe even the most dangerous ways of getting over a man.

We started living like a couple. I did not try to assess what, why, how, or when things had changed. Of course Zaid and I liked each other, but our relationship was circumstantial. We were both single, we were not answerable to anyone, and after what had happened, we just went with the flow.

Needless to add — the calls to his cabin stopped, and the boys who had discussed my probable bra size with him earlier, were just too embarrassed to even look him in the eye.

I told my parents I shared my apartment with him. Although they were not very happy about it, I was not exactly asking for their permission. I was old enough to live my life as I pleased. He too had told his family that he was living with me.

My parents were very worried because he was Muslim, but it was not something they would discuss with me. My brother and sister were usually the go-betweens.

'Is he just her flat-mate, or is he her room-mate?' my mother cautiously asked my sister, trying to make up her mind about what was worse — pre-marital sex, or a live-in relationship that I made no attempts to hide.

'Why don't you ask her yourself?' my sister replied.

My parents were thankful that I didn't live in Delhi, or any place where their gossiping family and friends had any chance of finding out about my lifestyle. This was something they could hide for as long as they wanted, and they hoped that sooner or later I would break up with him. And why not? The world does survive on hope, and they were entitled to theirs!

A few months later I got in touch with Suraj, just to make sure he was doing fine. He came home one evening. He checked out whatever he could to make a mental image of Zaid.

'Hey, I like his books and he listens to cool music. Seems like a great guy.'

I will never know if he was lying or telling me the truth, but I was at peace to have his approval. I was relieved to see him get his life back slowly. I wanted him to meet someone too, and fall in love again, so that the burden on my conscience would be lifted.

'Stay a little longer, and meet him before you go,' I said.

Maybe it would have been more reasonable to expect a snowstorm in Bombay in May, don't you think? Zaid was not possessive, and didn't mind at all that I was in touch with Suraj. Our relationship was based on freedom and acceptance. We both had lives of our own from the very beginning. His best friend from his college days in Delhi lived close by. By now I had spent over seven years in Bombay, and had a big bundle of friends. Despite the nature of our relationship, he did have an opinion on that.

Zaid was smart, and he knew it. He felt my friends didn't add any value to his life (or mine for that matter) — especially those without a B-school degree! And he believed I had too many friends for there to be any quality in my relationships. I didn't see Rima that often now, and I was still studying (though paying my own college fees). Work, college, and home took up most of my time. Rima was a successful architect, and travelled quite a bit too. Our lives chugged along. Zaid and I shared a comfortable relationship. There was no wild romance or crazy love. Rather, there was mutual admiration. He was somewhat the hero, and I undoubtedly the worshipper. Yet, it was a pretty democratic relationship.

Chapter 26

One Christmas, Zaid and I decided to go to Goa upon a whim. The world converges at Goa during this festive season. We had no hotel reservations, but we were confident we would manage *something*. After all, how difficult could it be to find one room?

Ah, it was not difficult... it was impossible.

Goa was infested with tourists crawling around the city like cockroaches, two of those being Zaid and me. We spent the entire first day looking for accommodation — just going from hotel to hotel. We went from optimism to pessimism, to worry, to desperation — all in a matter of a few hours. We called a friend whose family lived in Goa, and asked for suggestions (read: begged her to help). She 'suggested' that we go to her friend's grandmother's house, who rented out several rooms. We saw a ray of hope. Of course, once we reached there, we saw that the friend's friend's grandmother also had a houseful! But we looked so distressed that she offered us a single bed in her balcony, with access to the bathroom, at the princely amount of a hundred rupees a night. Since it was a covered balcony, I can say that we managed a roof over our heads. And that is how we spent our Christmas and New Year's eve that year.

We returned to Bombay on New Year's Day. Two days later, Zaid and I got married, exactly the day before I turned twenty-five. It happened on our way to office, wearing the clothes we wore to work. We stopped at the court, and registered our wedding.

I am not sure if this qualified as eloping because we were living on our own, and there was no one to run away from.

Except for the three witnesses, none of our other friends knew. We hoped for no drama... and it was almost like that. But Rima's father chose that very day to register her brother's wedding at the same court at the very same time.

Now, what was the probability of something like that happening in a city like Bombay? It was incredibly embarrassing to say the least, to be caught by her father, running away from no one getting married like that.

It was like any other day in my life. Zaid and I went to work after the wedding. Nothing changed — including our clothes or even our dinner plans for the rest of the day. I didn't change my name, and I never gave my changed marital status another thought. Even the thought of informing my parents didn't cross my mind. There was no one I wanted to share my world with.

Even later we didn't bother publicising our marital status. Our families rarely discussed the idea of us marrying each other. *Why ask and unnecessarily sow the seeds when they might be just contemplating breaking up?* I am sure they thought that.

My sister and I met often. But when, for a few days, I didn't hear from her, I found it odd. I went to her hostel to check on her. She was delirious, and running a high fever. Zaid put her on the first available flight to Delhi. My parents picked her up. She was diagnosed with tuberculosis. She took months to recover, and after she was better, she returned to Bombay to complete her studies. This time she stayed with us.

On the professional front, after working with the Taj for two years, I started getting bored. The Taj was not a company, it was an institution, and one in which you could easily get lost. A huge place. Everyone liked to hang around till late and look busy irrespective of whether they had work or not. Inspiration was hard to find. At least it was like that in the late '90s.

In any case, I always wanted more from life. Yes, excitement was lacking at my workplace. And though monotony was seeping into my bones now, I was attached to the place and the people. My office was located in the old wing of the magnificent Taj Mahal hotel and I had made some lovely friends. Gayatri and Roshini were my favourites.

The Taj sent me to Bali to attend a conference organised by a CRS Company. A CRS (Central Reservations System) was a piece of software that assisted travel agents with airline bookings. Though she was from Bombay, it was in Bali that I met Kamal for the first time. The travel industry is one of the few trades in the world that employs more women than men, but don't get fooled by that. Even today, most of the top jobs are taken by men. Kamal was just four years younger than my mother. Not only were there few working women from her generation, even fewer made it to the top. And she was one of them.

She was modern (she had married of her own choice), yet conservative (she wore only saris to work); she maintained a balance between work and home carefully, raising two amazing teenagers at the same time.

Kamal was the general manager of this CRS Company, and offered me a job with more responsibility and more money — a lethal combination almost impossible to resist. So I took it up.

Working with her was so much more personal. She did all the things most women bosses do — invited us to her place, made work fun, and even offered us motherly advice when she felt we needed it. Though I had already been working for five years before I met her, I was still a piece of damp clay that could be moulded into any shape. And I should give her credit for chiselling me a bit.

We challenged each other's ideas, and she allowed me the space and freedom to grow. She taught me two important lessons I would have never learnt in any management school. First: *Have a brain? Use it.* She didn't want us to be just doers, she wanted us to be thinkers. The second lesson: *Have a voice? Speak up.* She believed that if we had conviction in our ideas, we could swim upstream. We were a small team, and she brought out the best in all of us.

Zaid and I had still not announced we were married. It was a strange marriage. We both lived marooned on our own island, not connected with the rest of the world. Our parents still resisted the idea of us being together, and my mother tried her very best to make sure that we split up. But I always found out her tricks. She always denied them. She tried niceness as a strategy, but I was too clever to fall for it. This was an aspect of my parents I hadn't seen before. Not liking a boyfriend was one thing, but plotting a break up was quite another — like adding red-hot chillies in someone's dessert!

I started trusting her even less than before. I wasn't financially dependent upon them anyway, and now I also started losing my emotional dependence on them. Then, quite suddenly, they agreed to accept the imminent marriage.

One of my brother's friends, a smart boy of course, had put the proposition forward in such a manner that any self-respecting parent living in Delhi would accept it.

'Imagine if she were to run away and get married.' Of course in a way I had already done so.

The shame of a Muslim son-in-law would be less damaging than the shame of a daughter running away and getting married. The former would reflect on me, while the latter would reflect on them.

It was all very dramatic. Naturally, my parents were bothered about what others, especially their own families, would say. Marrying a boy of my choice was a blemish on my character. And now I had disregarded all social standards set and followed by the Punjabis of the world, and taken it to another level by marrying a Muslim!

Eventually, I suppose I would go back to my world leaving them in theirs, and this was their life — they talked about other people and now other people would talk about them. And I had put them in that position. But my parents pretended not to be bothered, and tried to look happy throughout, even though my wedding card sounded a bit like a public apology.

Chapter 27

Zaid dealt with his family, and a date was fixed for the 'social' wedding. But strange things began to happen just before that.

Zaid's office was celebrating an important occasion, and the entire team had been invited with their companions. I was more than Zaid's companion. I was his live-in girlfriend, who was secretly also his wife, on the verge of becoming his spouse publicly. So I was on the guest list.

Sitting at the bar with some of his colleagues, I saw him dancing with Maria. It was nothing like two colleagues dancing. She was all over him. And then I noticed her hand on his butt. Yes, he did have a cute butt, but that hardly gave anyone, except me, the right to allow their hands to land on it.

But, like a true Capricorn, I did not create a scene. On the contrary, I teased him about it.

'Why was she all over you?'

'She was just drunk. Her boyfriend did not show up for the party.'

Nothing happened after that for a couple of weeks. And then, out of the blue, at dinner a few days later, he told me that my friend Roshini from the Taj had called to ask him if he was seeing Maria.

'How odd. Why would she ask you that? She doesn't even know her!'

'I don't know, but you need to tell her this is our business.'

He looked really upset, and now I was mad at Roshini.

This was very tricky — not for me, but for Roshini. Just a few weeks ago a very good friend and I had been having a conversation about making the choice — to tell or not to tell. If you saw a friend's husband getting intimate with another woman, would you tell her?

Of course you would! We were women for God's sake! We would do our best to protect our friends. And what Roshini had done was even better — she had approached him and not me!

Yet, I called her the next morning and asked her what she had said to him.

'Everyone says he is having an affair with Maria, Gauri. You are my friend. I am just looking out for you.'

'I don't need your protection, Roshini, and he is not having an affair with her. I insist you call and apologise to him.'

She was embarrassed that I had called her and given her a piece of my mind. Why would I do that to someone who was trying to help me? Ironically, again, because I am a woman. I trusted my man, and above all, this was my business. My friends' business could be my business, but my business was not their business. It's complicated, I know, but at times that's exactly how we women are!

'I am very sorry,' she said.

Three weeks — yes, not months but weeks — before our social wedding, Zaid started acting strange.

'Do we need to have a social wedding? I don't like this drama. It's better if we just keep it between us.'

'What do you mean?' I asked, thinking that maybe all men who are about to be married asked their to-be-wife this question.

'You know, if something happens between us, it would be so much more difficult if our families were involved. It would be simpler if it were just you and me.'

'Like what?' I still couldn't understand what he was saying.

'Like if it doesn't work out, and we want to go our own ways at some point.'

Yes, we women are complicated. But I knew I wanted to get married when I wanted to get married. If I didn't, I would have broken up months in advance. I wouldn't have chickened out three weeks before the wedding!

'Why would we want to do that?' I asked him.

'I don't know. I have been thinking lately that maybe marriage is not for me. I don't want to live a predictable life — become a middle-aged parent with an overweight wife, and have kids bawling all over the place. I want to be able to live out of a suitcase. If I want to go on a vacation, I should be able to pick up my bags and go. I like my freedom.'

'Isn't it a bit late for you to want that? Why are you getting cold feet?'

He knew we were already married, our social marriage was a farce. What was he talking about?

'I am telling you, it will be very complicated once the families are involved.'

He was saying things that made no sense to me, and his behaviour was even more aberrant. Maybe he was on drugs.

Then a stray thought found its place in my vocal cords.

'Is it Maria?'

There was silence.

'Look, I get it. Outsiders misunderstand relationships, but this is your moment. If you are seeing her, tell me now.'

He started crying. 'No I am not, and I am sorry I am doing this to you.'

'What are you doing to me?'

'We will get married.'

I thought about Hiten for a fleeting moment, except that I was already Zaid's wife. I was too dumb to realise he wasn't hundred per cent sure he wanted to be with me, and he was too spineless to walk out.

Chapter 28

And, with this as the backdrop to our social wedding, we were announced man and wife for the world to know. We took off from work for exactly a week. I had the chance to meet his sister from New York. She and Suraj's father shared their birthday, and I loved her instantly. She was soft-spoken, and delicately beautiful with sharp features. She was the quiet rebel.

I had always wanted to visit the US — to see Chicago from the top of the Sears Tower. I had tried to go to the US the previous year, but I didn't because my mother had given me a lengthy lecture on how I was wasting my money.

'You could buy a nice television and a refrigerator with this money. When will you ever learn to save? Spending money on travel is like throwing it in a flowing river… you get nothing back.'

'But the experience and the memories stay with you forever,' I argued.

Oh, we argued and fought all the time.

Finally, I had to call the trip off, even though my tickets had been issued. I didn't like all this fighting, and I was sure that now that we had had this discussion, Murphy's Law would kick in and something would go wrong with the trip. So I bought a refrigerator and a television with the money — something I could touch and admire. I would stick my head into the fridge during the Bombay summer to take in the cool air and convince myself that it was worth it.

My parents arranged two big dinner parties to celebrate our wedding. Most of their family and friends — some of whom had seen me grow up, and some I had never seen in my life — came to see me and my Muslim husband.

Nicky was still living in Delhi, but despite our close friendship over the past several years, he didn't come for my wedding. He made work an excuse that I didn't buy. I think he was trying to show solidarity with Suraj. It was something that stayed unsaid, but understood.

Zaid's parents too arranged a wedding reception at their home in Assam. I had the opportunity to meet his extended family. They had all come to see his Hindu wife who, they hoped, would turn Muslim one day. For a few weeks my parents and I had a peaceful and amicable relationship. After all, *they* had made the ultimate sacrifice.

Zaid and I came back to our home, and routine, in Bombay — spending close to three hours a day commuting and most of our waking hours at work. I would head to college after work and reach home well past dinner time. My weekends were taken up by homework, assignments, and extra classes. At some point, I started noticing that Zaid was returning later than me on most evenings.

'How come you are working late these days?' I asked.

'What do I come home to? You are busy with college all the time.'

'I have been in college since we met — it's nothing new in our lives! Anyway, I have just a few more months to go.'

'Did I say that I have a problem with it? I am just answering your question.'

To make it up to him, I decided to keep myself free that Saturday. He bought two tickets for a play based on Khalil Gibran's book *The Prophet*. It turned out to be a monologue by one actor. All was well, till the lights were turned off. And then, a strategic audience spotlight came on. It was right on me! Now, I had read the book and I had loved it, but for some reason listening to one actor for two hours made me yawn a lot!

'You just don't know how to appreciate art!' he said on our

way home.

Of course, he was embarrassed — he was married to the woman the whole world saw yawn through a critically acclaimed play.

'It has nothing to do with appreciating art — listening to one voice for that long is like listening to a lullaby.'

'He is an award winning actor!'

'So? I am still entitled to my own opinions — not everyone loves every actor who's won an Academy Award, do they?'

'You know, you and I are just so not "we"!'

'Where did that come from? Just because you choose a play that I don't end up appreciating means that we are not "we"? How about we are so not "we" because you are out drinking with some boys who don't matter to our lives.' I didn't think he was working twelve hours a day every evening that he came home late.

'They are my friends.'

'Really? Well, you are suddenly doing pretty well for someone who is not social.'

Maybe I should have paid more attention to every one of his words and actions, but I dismissed it as just one of those things! Two people, strong individuals — living under the same roof for a lifetime are not exactly going to agree with everything, are they? Hell, my sister and I who got along so well fought and argued, but that didn't for a moment mean that we didn't love each other!

One day my sister spotted him in a pub with Maria. He had not expected to see her there.

'Where is Gauri?' she marched up to him and asked.

'I don't know,' he replied. 'Meet Maria. She and I work together. We just got off work.'

'It's 2.00 am on a Friday night, and you don't know where your wife is?' Like hell my sister was going to make small talk! She paid her bill and walked away, as Zaid looked on.

The next morning he volunteered the information to me. Now, this was totally out of character because he had long stopped telling me where he was going or with whom. So I came up with the most logical question: 'Why are you telling me this?'

Sometimes, we women are really smart!

'Oh, hasn't Nandini told you about it already?'

So, he was guilty.

My sister had stopped telling me things about him after seeing how I had humiliated Roshini.

'You are blind,' she had told me.

But today, on 11 July, 1998, he told me who he had been out with. I had been to the temple the previous evening with Gayatri, and she had told me to ask God to help me. While I was praying, he had been with Maria at the pub. And at some unearthly hour, alone in our bedroom, I had reached out for his bag, and turned its contents over on the bed. And amongst them were two neatly folded letters from Maria.

They were classic syndromes, really — faceless friends, a social life you didn't know about, and places you hadn't heard of, a schedule you couldn't keep track of, a mention of restaurants you had never been to together. I had nothing but my inexperience and blind faith to blame for not having recognised the signs.

Yes, the world already knows, but you are always the last one to know.

I had just had a wedding reception four months ago. I was twenty-six years old, and I had gone against everything and everyone to be with this man.

I needed to tell someone. I found myself banging on my sister's door. She opened it, half asleep, wondering why I was behaving like a possessed woman at that hour. There was something about the look on my face that made her grab the letters from my hand, and without reading them, she knew exactly what was going on.

'It's the middle of the night. Get some sleep. We'll see what's to be done tomorrow morning.'

'I don't want to sleep in this house. I don't want to sleep on this bed. I don't want to be here at all!'

Eventually, we went over to a friend's place for the night.

Later, Gayatri would tell me that she had seen him and Maria kissing the week before, and that was why she had taken me to the temple, so that I could really ask God to help me, just in case my hotline was not clear enough. A few days after I had found the letters I called Roshini.

Of course she forgave me. We were all women after all!

Chapter 29

I remembered God. That's one of the cool things about a relationship with God. He is so undemanding — a bit like the fireman. You contact Him only when there is a fire, and He doesn't mind. I have to admit that for a while I was mad even at Him. I mean I trusted Him to make things better for me, but He just didn't seem to be focusing on the task.

The next morning I was numb and had a dull headache. My mind was blank. When I was younger, I had imagined I would be many things... but not once did I think that I would be the wife of a man who was two-timing her.

I called Zaid from my friend's place the next morning. It was Sunday.

'Please, just come back home. I will explain. It is not like it looks,' he pleaded.

Not like it looks? I wanted to hear that story.

Anyway, that was my home and all my things were there — from my toothbrush to my ex-boyfriend's stuffed toy, to the most expensive jewellery my mother had given me on my wedding. So I went back.

He was crying. As soon as I reached home, he hugged me.

'Don't touch me!'

I was not crying, but I was angry and my face revealed my feelings clearly.

He told me how difficult the past few months had been

because he and I were so busy with our lives. He said he and Maria had grown close because they spent more time with each other at work. According to him, he and I had lost our togetherness. 'If you were in my place you would do the same.'

'I am in the same place every day. I have more opportunities than you do. All I need to do is say the word, but I don't do it.'

'She is not like that,' he said. 'She reads the same books I read, she listens to the same music I do.'

I was not going to sit there and have him justify himself and paint this picture of benevolence in front of me.

'I don't care. As far as I am concerned, she is just a slut.'

Till then I didn't believe that people could change overnight. I had died the first time I moved to the hostel, but this time, it was a darker death. It was not the thought that he was with another woman that hurt, it was the loss of trust that changed things for me. Overnight, my new motto became *Guilty unless proven Innocent*. And it applied to everyone who came my way.

I called his sister in New York, and told her about Maria. It upset her too. She asked me who his friends these days were.

How would I know? I was the wife!

I called my parents and told them.

'We knew this would happen.'

Yeah, yeah, yeah, what else could I expect?

My sister's support to me was critical. She kept the peace with my parents, and was the only person in my family I could depend on for any emotional backup. But she had started to loathe Zaid. We could not have a conversation without her cutting him up to pieces. My brother and I mostly pretended that nothing was going on in my life.

And how did I feel about Zaid? Unsure! As in… I didn't know how I should feel about him after this happened, but somehow, I didn't hate him. When I married him, I did love him. And I did love him even the day I found the letters, but the way he had been behaving before that had changed things a bit. I had begun to see him less as a hero and more as a confused man.

I called Rima to tell her. Her brother picked up the phone and told me she had gone to the US.

'Well, could you just let her know that I am in a soup?'

'What sort of soup? Can I help?'

'Not really.'

I told him what had happened. He came to see me that evening. Rima called me from the US.

I remembered a time just after college when I had got chicken pox, and had to move out of the hostel for two weeks. I could not even get a train or plane home because it was contagious. I had nowhere to go to, and I had called Rima. Without hesitation, she had asked me over and let me stay at her place. This time I felt I had emotional chicken-pox. I really missed her.

As my friends got to know, they were shocked. Zaid was unmistakably a 'nice guy'. They all liked him. He was just not the sort of person they could see doing something like this.

'He's made a mistake... it will be okay,' they told me.

Some friends advised me to give him a chance, and some told me to break up with him. Some told me to stand up and 'fight' for him, and some told me to call Maria and shred her to pieces. Everyone was full of advice. They were just trying to help.

Ironically, Zaid's thesis on quantity and quality of friends was grossly flawed. There is a direct correlation between what you sow and what you reap, when it comes to investing emotions in human relationships. I was surrounded by dependable people, and I got support from each one of them. This circle of friends was my biggest strength.

Chapter 30

Suraj learnt about it too, and came to see me at my house. He had bought me a Cadbury's Dairy Milk bar — my favourite chocolate. I put on my bravest look for him.

'How are you?'

'I am fine.'

'Well, you shouldn't be at this point. Your life is on the verge of falling apart,' he said. 'But I want you to know that I am here for you if you need anything. I mean *anything* at all. You want to speak to someone, call me — no matter what time it is... you need money, ask me...you need something done, tell me, okay?'

'Okay.'

What was he doing here? Why had he come? My brain was talking to itself again.

'You are the smartest girl I know, so I don't need to tell you what you should do. But I will tell you this — you are answerable to no one but yourself,' he said.

It was the same thing Rima had said to me. Their support was unconditional and complete. We all need *one* person in our life on whom we can rely completely, with no strings attached. I had more than one. And I had my sister.

'God is doing this because I broke your heart so badly,' I started to cry.

I truly believed this was my karma catching up with me. I regretted the way I had treated him, and he had no reason whatsoever to be nice to me.

'It doesn't work like that. Things just happen, Gauri. That's life.'

'I never thought this would ever happen to me,' I sobbed.

'It depends on the way you look at it. Count your blessings.'

'Do you still love me?' I have no idea where that came from; it just popped out of my mouth when it shouldn't have.

He thought for a moment. 'You and I were *we* at another time and place.'

That made me feel infinitely better. He hadn't said 'yes', but he hadn't said 'no' either.

'Then why are you here?'

'I had to be here. I owed it to you. I was never there for you when we were together. If I had been there for you then, this wouldn't have happened, right?' He was smiling at his own joke.

I knew that day that a part of me would always love him — till I died.

Suraj told Nicky about my situation, and he phoned me from Delhi. Can you believe that we didn't talk about Zaid at all?

He was still flogging tractors, so he told me about his last visit to some village whose name I couldn't even pronounce.

He said he had seen his tractor being pulled by two cows because the village had run out of fuel! He told me some more stories that I don't quite think were true, but they did make me forget for a little while that I was supposed to be devastated about my two-timing husband.

The next few days were routine. I went to work as usual, I did not tell anyone at office about my personal problems.

Work was a great escape, and the ten to twelve hours I was there, I didn't think about home.

Rayo invited me over to a very fancy restaurant to lift my spirits, with spirits! I really liked the idea of having a friend from my parents' generation.

'Is love permanent, Rayo? Do you still love your wife?' I asked him.

She is beautiful even today. I am sure she must have been a show stopper in her younger days. They had met at work, and he had married her when they were both in their twenties.

'Of course I do... very much, but when you have been married for more than two decades, love changes. It is not the same type of love when you are young. You will understand it when you are closer to my age,' he said as honestly as he could. That was something I could always trust Rayo to be — honest.

'No, tell me now. How?'

He thought for a moment. 'You know, when you are young, love is like a firecracker — dazzling, bright, and electric. When you are older, it's like a candle. It gives light and warmth and lasts much longer.'

He was right. It was a complicated type of love I didn't understand at twenty-six.

Zaid came home early every day of that week. He said he was sorry, and tried to make up, but he was still seeing Maria at work every day. I was not interested in his apologies.

And then came his birthday. I decided to let bygones be bygones, albeit only for a day. I went to see him at his office after work. It was very late, and he didn't expect me there. I wanted to surprise him.

Now, let me offer some free advice if, God forbid, you ever need it. When your spouse is having an extra-marital affair, the worst thing that you can do to yourself (and I am specific here — not to them, but yourself) is to *surprise* them with normal things.

I walked in, and noticed there was no one around. Then I saw the two of them. She saw me first and froze. That was the only eye contact I ever had with her. He was sitting on her table, bent over her intimately. He had his back to me, so he could not see me. She nudged him.

I felt sick in my stomach. That was the moment when I realised what it meant to have a heartache. It was almost a physical pain — a little bit like someone grabbing my heart in his palms and squeezing it — very slowly, a dull pain, not a sharp one, a pain that would stay for a very long time.

I ran down four floors, and he followed me. Ever since I had found out about them, I had never wept uncontrollably.

But now I was crying like a baby, and felt like one. I felt lonely, abandoned, and unloved.

I wanted my mother to hug me and tell me she loved me. For some strange reason I thought of Kamal. She knew nothing of what was going on, but I called her. I was sobbing. She asked me over to her house. That day Kamal was the mother in whose arms I could cry. Her kids started and finished their dinner, then their homework, and even went to bed, and I was still crying.

And, eventually, everyone in my office got to know.

Chapter 31

Almost three weeks had gone by since I had discovered the letters. I was still trying to absorb what had happened.

Maybe I even imagined at some point that he and I would get over it, and go on being together till one of us died — like married couples did.

But there was more to this story. Maria too had a boyfriend she had been seeing for years before she started going out with Zaid. His name was Sameer. After I found out about Maria and Zaid, Maria had told Sameer about Zaid as well. Now that it was out in the open, everyone knew about everyone else. There was turmoil in everyone's life. It was a very complicated situation that was just about to get worse.

One day, Sameer and two of his friends went on an all-boys picnic. Ignoring the safety instructions, one of them went for a swim in the pond. He began to drown. Sameer jumped in to save him. They were both sucked inside. They were my age — twenty-six. Later in the evening, Zaid received a phone call, and told me he had to go.

'You should.' I simply could not comprehend what Sameer's family must be going through, and how Maria might be feeling. I could only sympathise with her. She would now have to live the rest of her life knowing that she would never have the opportunity to make it up to Sameer. I hadn't thought anything worse could happen when I found Zaid cheating on me. But something worse had happened.

Zaid didn't come back the whole night.

I couldn't stop thinking about death. No matter what your story was, it ended someday. Sometimes — sooner than one expected. And the unpredictable nature of that end — particularly the un-timeliness of it, changed the way I looked at things. Knowing that young people died was one thing; knowing that a young person connected with you in some way had died was another. It was real. And these stray thoughts occupied my mind when Zaid was away that night.

He was absent all of the next day. And the following day.

'She is suicidal. I really need to be there for her,' he kept saying.

It was a very difficult situation. I could not be anything but compassionate towards this woman I didn't know, whose boyfriend had died, and who was in love with my husband. And where did that leave me?

Finally, I called him at work, and said that I hoped to see him home that evening. After five days of being away he came home.

'I just want to tell you that Sameer is gone, and I am very sorry for his family and Maria. But you do need to know that I am not dead. You cannot spend your life holding her hand because I too need someone to do that for me,' I said.

'I am sorry, I just need to sort some things out in my head.'

'You can do that, but not under my roof.'

He was taken aback. This was not just my roof, this was our home. We had built it together, filling it with things that made our memories — putting up pictures, buying furniture, things he liked, things I wanted. And I was now calling it 'my' roof.

'You want me to move out?' He sounded surprised.

'If you are not sure you want this, Zaid, and you need time to think, fine. But you can't do it here. You can't have your cake and eat it too.'

I could have left too, but it was unquestionably his mistake, and I would not inconvenience myself because of something he had done. It was fair.

Chapter 32

He found a place a few days later. I helped him pack like a mother would help a child going to school for the first time.

I allowed him to only take what belonged to him. I kept whatever we had bought for the house as a couple. I had bought him a fancy music system for his birthday that he wanted to take.

'I can't let you have it.'

'But it was a present. You bought it for me,' he protested.

'Well, I just changed my mind. Now it is mine.'

I had thought separating his things from mine after all this time together might be painful. But it was not. Though I did have a few moments of weakness during which I handed him my very favourite pillow. It was the one we always fought for.

'You are giving this to me?' he said with a look of pain on his face.

'You can have it.' I said with no emotion in my voice.

'Will you be all right?' he asked.

'Do I look like someone who can't take care of herself?' *Yeah, take a look at me, dude!* My mind started babbling!

I was indeed taken aback at how distant I could behave. I didn't know I had this ability to deal with difficult situations by simply blocking them out. The mind acts only with as much or as little power as you give it. I made mine the COO, and it was totally in-charge of my heart. It would not allow my feelings to wander anywhere close to negative emotions.

Another thought zipped through my head. Maybe I would have felt a bit better if I had slapped him. I had flung a pillow down on the bed in anger when I had found Maria's letters. That was the best I could get myself to do. Maybe, at times, I should have broken my non-violence vow, you know, just to feel good. Just one slap! But I could not do it.

Zaid and I had never changed the money system in the house. We still shared our expenses from the kitty. My friends used to find our arrangement odd, even funny, particularly after we were married. But it wasn't weird to us. We didn't think we had to do what others were doing and, with time, those had become the rules of our relationship.

Just after our social wedding we had moved to a larger apartment (read 'more rent'), and now my financial burden would increase. But luckily I was earning enough to take on that additional expense. Destiny had taken me to Bali where I had met Kamal, who had then offered me a job that not only paid me more, but also came with a boss in whom I had the perks of a part-time mother.

It was at some time during those days that my niece arrived into the world and so I went to see her over the weekend. My parents had tried to dissuade me from asking Zaid to leave. They were right, I suppose, in thinking that there would be less chances of repair if we were not together. And, of course, the possibility of divorce really scared them.

I remember accompanying my mother for an outing on that trip when she suddenly spotted some acquaintance approaching us from the opposite side. She grabbed my arm and said, 'Not a word on your separation.'

Even the thought of discussing my 'on-the-rocks' marriage with some vague person on the street had not crossed my mind, but something about how this situation had come up made me go so blank that I didn't register a word of the conversation that transpired between the two women. I tried to control my anger, to understand what would be an acceptable response to what she had just said.

'What is your problem really? I haven't committed a crime

that you need to be ashamed of me, you know. Nothing that's happening is my fault — it's just a bad situation, a bad relationship — it can happen to anyone... to someone who is married and someone who is not married!'

Think about it. In the Indian society, even now, the D-word is actually worse than the F-word, especially if you are a girl. Your life is finished if you are divorced because, if a couple divorces, it is the girl's mistake... naturally. If her man commits adultery, it is because she could not hold his attention. If he is a woman-beater, it is because she deserves it.

In fact, I realised what it means to be a divorcee only recently, when a much younger friend with a great job and a fabulous education was updating me about a common friend — a divorcee. She had married a man who hadn't been married before. She said something to the effect that it was her incredible luck that she didn't have to 'settle' for another divorced or widowed man since she was a divorcee herself. Yes, being divorced is like being born with two noses. *She is a freak.* How do the parents of such a freak step out of their homes without other people passing comments?

Until recently divorce was such a taboo that even our religion made no provisions for it in our lives. There were social rules for what must become of unmarried girls, and girls widowed, but divorcees? Are you kidding? Indian girls don't get a divorce; they suffer because that is the honourable thing to do. Why would anyone want a divorce?

And now, having had a live-in relationship or having chosen a Muslim spouse were small things compared to the possibility of a divorce. Ah yes, that would be another first.

How unfortunate for my parents! Why didn't they have a daughter who had other kind of firsts — going into space, getting a gold medal at the Olympics, or at least at Bombay University — or even the first to become a millionaire would have suited them fine!

So living at the epicentre of the world of Punjabi gossip — Delhi — it must have been a nightmare for my parents to have a child, let me correct that, a *daughter,* who was possibly going to get a divorce. But, I have to be honest, that thought had not yet crossed my mind.

I returned to my life in Bombay where no one had judged me when I was single or when I was someone's girlfriend, when I was living-in, when I was married and now when I was separated! The city was my haven.

One afternoon Kamal called me to her cabin, and asked me to shut the door behind me.

'Your parents called. You know, they are very worried about you. They are afraid you might do something drastic.'

'What did you say to them?' I asked her. My blood was boiling. Now they were even stalking my boss!

'I told them you are a very sensible girl, and they should be proud of you. I am proud of you. You are very young, and you are in a bad situation. Most people I know would be abusing Maria or creating scenes, but you conduct yourself with such dignity...'

At least some adult had some confidence in me!

'You should call them,' she said after a pause. 'They care about you.'

But I didn't. I dismissed that relationship.

Chapter 33

After Zaid left, the story became even more twisted. No, actually, it was my ovaries that became kind of twisted — with the weight of a cyst!

I was at a meeting one morning when I had an awful pain in my abdomen. And, when I got stuck at an angle of forty-five degrees, I called Kamal and told her I needed help. Even the damn cyst could not find a more suitable moment to make its presence felt!

Though the doctor said it was huge and would have to be operated, only when I saw the scan did I believe that he wasn't trying to con me into surgery! Remember? *Guilty unless proven Innocent!*

'It won't disappear with just medication,' he said. 'You will have stitches on your belly, and you won't be able to go to work for about a week.'

It was a weekend. No one could trace Zaid, but my friends were there for me. Someone came with the money, someone came with a car, someone else brought the food, and everyone took turns to babysit me. It was a minor surgery, but I was calculating how much of a financial setback it would turn out to be. And, that was not because I was a Punjabi!

My mother offered to come over, but I didn't want her anywhere near me. She was behaving like the victim. She had often told my sister how angry she was with Zaid.

'Look at what he has done to us!'

'What has he done to you, Mom? Whatever it is, it can't be worse than what he has done to Gauri,' my sister told her.

'First she goes and marries a Muslim boy, and now I hope she doesn't get divorced, because then we won't be able to face the world.' My mother even whined about the wedding expense. Now *that*, I think, was certainly because she was a Punjabi.

'This is not about you. This is about her life.'

I could overhear the conversation, and it was driving me nuts. I grabbed the phone.

'What is the problem? You are embarrassed that I might get a divorce?'

'Look, you are young and you don't understand. He is a man, and men are like that. Please realise that you are a *girl*. You need to forgive him and make it work.'

It was this phase of my life that completely damaged my already shaky relationship with my parents — you know, sort of pushed it over the cliff. I was angry that they hadn't protected me as a child; I was angry that they had always given precedence to their reputation over my feelings; I was angry that they always thought I should compromise because I was a girl. And, as I thought more about things, I realised that over the years my anger had turned to rage.

I didn't need this. Not now.

I stopped giving them any information about what I was doing, or how the situation was progressing. I stopped talking to them. I think I cut them off from my life for months, maybe even a year or more.

⁓

Rima had returned from the US. She dropped me home after my surgery.

'You know, Gauru, your life is not so bad. Imagine what you

would have done if you had a baby. Or if you didn't have a job. Maybe you should just accept that your relationship with your parents is something that cannot be improved in this lifetime.'

Yes, sometimes acceptance of such a fate is easier than fighting it. Why is it that we must have an ideal relationship with everyone? Why do we strive for our lives to be perfect? I counted my blessings and accepted that I had more than some, even though I had less than others. This theory of relativity is a very peaceful theory. Seriously, it's like a short person standing next to someone shorter so that he can feel tall. I like it.

Finally, two days after the surgery, Zaid found out and came home to see me. It was a little awkward because this was the first time we were meeting after he had left the house.

Should I be welcoming, like I am to my friends, or should I be mad at him? I tried to behave since he was my babysitter for the day, and I would have to rely on him for my errands. He tried to be nice.

'Do you want to read?' he asked.

'No.'

'Tell me what you want to do.'

'Let's play Scrabble.'

He raised his eyebrows. Why would he do that? A game of Scrabble was not just a game between us, it was a battle for power. He had an excellent vocabulary, and I always lost when we played. But today it was almost like a challenge. He was amused, like Hercules would be if he were challenged by a kitchen mouse.

He pulled out the Scrabble board.

God, please help me.

This was important.

When the game was over, we added our points. God had given me a chance so that I could say what I wanted to say.

'You know why I married you, Zaid? I married you because I always thought you were better than me in every way. I looked up to you. But now I know you are only smarter, not better, than I am.'

Yes, I had thought Zaid would be my 'better half'. Not that I ever felt I wasn't good enough by myself... but I had imagined that in our partnership of a lifetime, we would give and receive from each other what we didn't have. I had compared marriage to a long distance race that's always more fun with a partner — a partner who would push me to go the distance.

And as if my comment was incomplete without the declaration, I added, 'And you just got thrashed at a game of Scrabble.'

See, I told you, it wasn't just a game.

There was silence. And I felt good.

A few days later, out of the blue, someone from the administrative department at my office sent me a whole lot of paperwork to do. It was related to my surgery. The company had a policy of automatically providing medical coverage to all employees, and mine had been taken up just four days before my surgery — no kidding! I had every penny spent on my surgery reimbursed by the insurance company.

Chapter 34

Shiv and I had been classmates in the MBA class. We studied and did all our projects together. Shiv was a very composed person — a good Tamilian boy, with this sort of spiritual aura about him. I am sure his mother had sufficiently overloaded his brain with moral injections throughout his growing years. Yet, what I liked about him was that he was not that goody-goody all the time. He could carry a few evil thoughts without jeopardising his mother's teachings.

A few weeks later, I told Shiv about how I had been wondering if I should have slapped Zaid at least once.

'That would have made you a lowly person.'

'But I don't feel satisfied.'

'You don't have to hit people to get satisfaction,' he said.

'That's hypothetical because we would never really know, right? That moment has gone, and I will never know if it would have felt good or bad.'

He thought for a few minutes, and then spoke up again. 'Let me take you to the club tomorrow. We'll play a game.'

'What game?'

'It's a surprise,' he smiled.

The next day he introduced me to the game of squash. It was the ultimate release for anger. Like a therapy. Every time I hit the ball, it felt good.

'And you can imagine that the ball is any person you want it to be,' he joked.

Hitting the ball wasn't just making me feel good, it was also my anti-depressant. And so sports returned to my life.

Chapter 35

Zaid and I met from time to time, once every few weeks, always outside in a café or a restaurant. We didn't even speak on the phone very often. Our lives were chugging along two different tracks. Neither of us knew if those tracks would intersect again. We both realised that we had travelled so far without giving anything, particularly our relationship, any thought, so some amount of introspection, at least now, was necessary.

'So, how is all your thinking going?' I asked him one afternoon. It was a few months since we started living apart.

'I feel you and I want different things from life,' he said.

'Like what?'

'You want a family, kids, and all that... I am not sure that's what I want. It's not about Maria.'

'You know, the life you describe to me — all this living out of a suitcase and all that — let me tell you, all men want it. All men are nomads. You are not alone. But sensible men understand that giving up this freedom is necessary for the higher experiences in life.'

'Higher experiences in life?' He started laughing. He was mocking me.

He was doing it again — displaying his sense of superiority.

I had to give him an analogy he would relate to.

'You did an MBA in marketing because you wanted to be

a Marketing Manager. But now you are the General Manager. You enjoyed your earlier job profile more, but now that you've been promoted, apart from looking into marketing, you need to handle a bit of HR, a bit of accounting, budgeting, operations, some administration work etcetera, right? Giving up your bachelorhood for the new experiences that marriage brings is just the same.'

'Maybe I am not cut out for this sort of thing. I don't know! I think of you. I can talk to her about things I can't talk to you about, but she doesn't give me the warm fuzzy feeling you do,' he said.

'In life, you will never get everything (borrowed from Rima, of course). The perfect marriage and the perfect spouse don't exist,' I said.

'Then people should just marry anyone on the street.'

'The thing is that there are no guarantees — in life or marriage.'

My sister was very annoyed with all these meetings I had with him.

'Why do you need to see him? He is just a loser.'

'I have so many friends I can talk to. He doesn't have anyone.' It was true.

'Why do you care how he solves his problems?'

'I do, because I am involved. Unless I speak to him, I will never know what is going on in his mind. He needs therapy, but doesn't know it.'

'And you are giving him therapy?' she asked.

'No, seeing him gives *me* therapy.'

Every time I met him, our conversations helped me clear my own head. I still didn't know what I wanted from this relationship and, for a Capricorn, this can be very distressing. We do not like the lack of clarity in anything — particularly in life and yes — in drinking water!

Chapter 36

My sister was studying to become a counsellor. I always felt that my meetings with Zaid were comparable to the counselling sessions she described — short, to the point, and with a gap between each meeting. Every time we met, there was something to reflect upon.

At each meeting I was able to detach myself a bit more and gain objectivity. It was as if I was a part of a big painting — a Picasso piece — yes, those are really complicated. After the meeting, I was able to step outside and see the big picture — through his eyes, and my own.

We met for lunch another day. He gave me a poem he had written about me. It looked quite original... I think I still have it somewhere.

'Have you never been attracted to other men since we met?' he asked me once.

Of course I was attracted to other men! I met attractive men all the time. They didn't all look like Greek gods, but they were mentally and emotionally stimulating, and that was sexier than guys who looked good, but couldn't make conversation. Sometimes they were older, sometimes they were younger, but we connected at some level. I enjoyed flirting, and it wasn't all meaningless. It made me feel attractive and energised me.

I remembered a trip to Hong Kong a couple of months earlier. I had gone to attend a travel conference. On the last day there was a dinner hosted at The Peak. It was one of the city's highest points, with a spectacular view. In the evening one could see the entire city's skyline, with little ferries and boats dotting the pier. The ambience was romantic. My high-heel shoes were killing me. The pain we women can go through for the sake of fashion is unbelievable.

I found a spot where I could sit comfortably. I had not noticed a good-looking man next to me. Out of courtesy, especially since he was at this table before me, I smiled at him. He introduced himself with his business card. I noticed he lived in Paris. I didn't give him my card. I was in no mood to socialise at the end of a three-day long event through which I had talked non-stop.

'It is nice to meet you, Leonardo.'

'Where are you from?'

'India.'

'Your accent — it's a bit English.'

It's funny how many people think Indians can't speak good English.

'And your accent is... so French.' I smiled. International opening flirting lines, like *what's your sunsign!*

'I am Italian, actually,' he grinned.

Oops! Faux pas.

I started laughing.

Italian men are my ultimate romantic heroes. My travel adventures had given me the chance to meet several, and I had stereotyped them. They would always hold the door for you, they knew how to roll out the red carpet, they always smelt good, they paid so much attention to your feelings that you might actually end up thinking that they had an interest in your life — and maybe they do. They would make the effort to look good just for you, and they would never shy away from calling you 'bella' even if you were the worst-dressed woman in the world. Actually, I don't think anything like that exists for them. Only an Italian would translate an entire Italian menu for you into English.

An Italian friend who has lived in India for over a decade, and whom I call Bello, once explained why Italian men have perfected the art of flirting. In Italy, apparently, men have to earn their women, in contrast to Indian men to whom a woman is given on a platter by her father.

Italian charm is irresistible, and as a girl who had been roughed up on the football field for a good part of her life, Italians appeal to my most deprived romantic senses as an irreplaceable species.

So he was Italian. That caught my fancy.

'So, are you too, like all Italian men, a Mama's boy?' I teased him.

Yes, all Italian men love their mothers. It is all part of the charm because, after all, mama is also a woman.

'I am. I mean I was — until she died.'

We had barely met a few minutes ago, and already we were exchanging details about our family. He was from Lucca, a tiny village tucked away in the Tuscan region. He had been the only child to his parents, and now both of them were gone. Their house in Italy still existed, but without the parents, it was not home to him. He was single (and very available). We spoke of death and what it did to those who were left behind. I told him about my relationship with my parents and how, even though my parents were alive, I felt they were hardly there for me.

We both had so many questions unanswered, and so many wounds unhealed. So we were spiritual partners — orphans. Something bound us together. And though we spoke of dark and painful things, it was a deep conversation.

Amidst two hundred people at that dinner, we didn't notice another person. Wine kept coming, food was served, but we didn't move from where we were sitting. Hours went by, and finally we had to take the last tram downtown. I walked barefoot, holding my shoes (he had even offered to hold them for me), and he walked with me. We reached my hotel, and it was time to say goodbye. I gave him a hug, and then very spontaneously there was a kiss, a quick peck on the lips. And then he went back to his hotel, and I went up to my room.

Would you believe it if I told you we never met again?

He didn't have my number or address, and although I remembered him for a very long time and that evening would remain fresh in my memory forever, I never wrote to him. Why? Because there was nothing more to write. Yet, for those few hours, we were connected in a way that poles of two magnets are. It was beautiful.

'Of course I have. I travel much more than you do, and I get to meet people all the time,' I replied to Zaid, remembering the handsome, scrumptious Leonardo.

'Where do you draw the line? How do you know it won't get out of hand?'

'Because I know when to stop.'

I think he was looking for answers himself, maybe a justification for what had happened.

'So emotional, mental or spiritual involvement is acceptable, but physical sex is not?' Before I could answer he added, 'I just don't think man was meant to be monogamous.'

'Yup… could be true, but I believe in marriage… and trust. That's why we got married. But you lied to me… and that is cheating.'

There are many happily married couples for whom monogamy is not part of the agreement. It is understood that they will do whatever they want to do. Some married men sleep with other women, and some women have sex with other men, but those are the rules of *their* relationship. These were not the rules of *our* relationship.

It was true that I was attracted to other men. And though I wasn't always able to control my feelings, I always had control over my actions.

Another thing about Maria that attracted Zaid was her mother. She was a famous social activist, and I was amused to learn that she fought for women's rights. It impressed him, he was in awe of her. She was trying to change the world, and he was all set to play his part.

'So what does her mother have to say about this whole situation?' It was an irresistible question.

'What do you mean?'

'You know what I mean. Daughter of a famous women's rights activist — a home breaker?'

Yes, I said it. And I loved saying it.

'She knows you and I already had trouble before she entered the picture.'

'Oh, did we? I had no idea before I saw her squeezing your butt that we had any trouble.'

A few weeks later my sister left for the US to see her boyfriend, who was studying in Los Angeles. I hated being alone.

The mornings were the most difficult. Once I started my day, and put on my proverbial roller-skates, I was zipping all day and it didn't matter. On most evenings I was too tired to think or brood.

The doors of my house were always open. Fresh air and good friends never ceased flowing in. Suraj dropped in one evening.

'What are you up to?'

'Just enjoying my own company.' I had Bryan Adams blaring on the same music system I hadn't allowed Zaid to take with him.

'You are drinking alone?' he said as soon as he laid his eyes on my glass. He sounded irritated.

'It's only my second drink. I am not drinking like I have a drinking problem.' I couldn't understand why he was making this big fuss.

'Losers drink alone.' Now he sounded more than just irritated. 'I don't like this,' he continued angrily, 'I don't like what you are doing to yourself, and what you are becoming.'

'I am not doing anything,' I shot back, 'and you no longer have the right to be bothered about what I make of myself.'

For a few seconds he didn't know how to react. I wanted to take it back. How could I say something like that to *him?*

Even an apology couldn't make up for something like that.

'I didn't mean that...'

Suddenly the look on his face changed, the anger disappeared.

'You want to drink? Let's go to a pub and drink. Not like this,' he said in a tone that indicated he had forgiven me because he understood.

What the hell was wrong with me?

After that evening, whenever I didn't like being alone I would go to the movies, at times by myself, and one day I even took a bus all the way to the other end of town and back — just to kill time.

I bought myself a copy of *Letters from a Father to his Daughter* by Jawaharlal Nehru and, only after I started reading it, I learnt that it was a textbook for Bombay University students studying History.

As time went by, my mind became clearer and clearer. But, initially, every morning I woke up with a sense of confusion. *Would I be married or would I be single after today? Where would life take me after this sunrise?*

Why was I still meeting Zaid? Why didn't I leave him like I had asked Jigna to leave Hiten, especially since this was not the mad, crazy love of my life? Why had I still not filed for divorce? I figured that just like you shouldn't get married unless you are hundred per cent sure, you should get a divorce only when every drop of your blood wants it. I wasn't waiting for him to come back, I was only waiting for myself to set me free.

One day when we met, Zaid said, 'We can make it work, but she will still be my friend; I will not stop being friends with her.'

What a joke!

Chapter 37

And so a whole year went by since I first found the letters. I decided not to renew the lease for the house. After all this time I was not sad to leave the place that was by now associated with so many memories. I wondered why. I saw my move to a new house as symbolic, like shutting the doors on a past life and moving on to another.

That was when I bravely decided to get my wisdom tooth pulled out. The tooth had been bothering me for months.

This was the worst pain I had ever experienced. Only a person who has been through a toothache can empathise with this. The dentist had told me to get it extracted. Apparently, nothing else can be done about a wisdom tooth until our species discards this feature in the process of evolution (in the next few thousand years), and what happens then is of no interest to me. I care a lot more about how I have to live my life during the next forty years — what the price of onions would be, what we will do as water becomes scarce...

The dentist had warned me it would be very painful. And I was so afraid of the pain! Pain makes me cry. Even a headache can make me cry. I didn't know then if he was just a bad dentist, or if there were really limited options to get teeth extracted — none of them painless. Later I found out that there really were no painless options those days, and I was also convinced that he wasn't just a bad dentist — he was terrible!

With my mouth swollen and gums stitched up, I went to my old house. I did not take a painkiller. I wanted to feel the pain. I wanted it to ache so much that I would not be able to tell the difference between heartache and toothache. Yes, it was a sort of self-invented therapy.

I sat alone in my old house and cried. I think I had always wanted to cry like that. And now, the wisdom tooth had given me the excuse. I cried for a very long time because I knew that after that day I would never cry for Zaid again.

That night I slept in my new house. I woke up the next morning with my head crystal clear. I knew what to do and I had the courage to do it, but I did not do it immediately. I went about my daily routine for the next few days.

Lakshmi continued to work for me in my new house. She was the one I depended on so that I could have a life outside my home. She would occasionally update a 'disinterested' me about how the man-hunt was progressing, and how the marriage 'deal' always fell through — over money of course. The search for a suitable husband for her had begun when she was just sixteen, even though it is illegal to marry off a girl of that age in India.

She and I were not exactly friends, but without having ever asked her, I knew she had a very good idea about what was going on in my life. I mean, what kind of IQ does it take to figure out why a married woman has no men's clothes or things in her house?

My new apartment was on the second floor in a lovely, quiet corner of Bombay. Yes, a place like that existed. There was a beautiful old tree in the garden, and the branches faced the balcony. This was my favourite part of the house. When it rained, I sipped my chai here, and I could see the rain pitter-patter on the leaves. I could smell the wet soil.

Then Zaid's sister called from New York and told me she was rushing to Assam. Zaid's mother was on her deathbed. We all prayed she wouldn't suffer. She died the next day. I booked the next flight to Assam, to be there with his sister and the rest of the family. Nothing that had happened was their fault. I had always had their support, and this was my chance to show them mine.

Two days later I returned to Bombay. Zaid stayed back with his family a bit longer. About a week later he called, and told me he would be returning by a certain flight. I went to pick him up at the airport, and brought him home. It was late evening. Both of us were tired. No one spoke about anything.

The next morning he made me some tea. We were sitting in the balcony. There was no pitter-patter, but the tree was full and green, and tiny sparrows came and went — as though playing kho-kho.

We sat listening to the chatter of the birds. After a very long time, he spoke up. 'Why did you bring me here?'

'Because I didn't want you to be alone at your place after you returned. I am sorry you lost your mother.'

He had been the apple of his mother's eye. It had been very difficult for her to deal with the fact that her favourite son, who could do no wrong, had done what he had. And he knew that.

'I am sorry for my mistakes. Can you please give me another chance?'

'We don't have to have to discuss this now, you know.'

He had just come back from his mother's funeral. I took a deep breath and closed my eyes, wishing that this conversation would end. There was a pregnant pause.

'No, I want to talk about it now. I am very sure. This is what I want.'

I pushed my hair behind my ears. I looked him straight in the eye. 'But it's not what I want. I don't want to be with you.'

He looked very confused. He hadn't expected it. 'Then... why did you do this? Why did you come to Assam? Why did you bring me to your house yesterday?'

'Because I am a better person, because it was the right thing to do, and because I would do it for anyone, not just you.'

It was my decision. I had mourned the death of this relationship during the time I was alone. There was no heartbreak.

It is always easier to deal with something when the decision is your own. I didn't love him anymore. Worse, I didn't respect him. Now I felt free and light. It would take six months for my divorce to come through.

Chapter 38

The months before that were filled with pain and sadness, but most of all I was angry with life. I was the volcano that was ready to blow up and I did — fairly often. Sometimes at my friends, my colleagues, my sister — I just needed the slightest instigation to erupt. But it is the mountain's own lava that destroys it. I felt heavy — as if the weight of the world was on my soul. I yearned for a quiet stillness. Upon someone's advice I joined a yoga class. It works for the whole world, even the westerners were embracing it. But it didn't work for me. Maybe that happened because I never took it seriously — I couldn't control my laughter if someone let out a funny squeak from the wrong end while doing an asana. When the class meditated, I would have an eye open to check how many were really focused on the task and how they looked. And, my body — maybe like my mind was just too inflexible to do most of the asanas! I was the wrong candidate and that sucked. I was even failing at yoga and that made my life look worse. Maybe if I was more spiritual, more believing in some way, things could have looked better.

All through that year I silently asked myself, *Why me?* Why did I have to go through that pain? I had read about suffering and pain making you a better person. Trust me, it's absolute hogwash; they say that stuff only to make you feel better. There is nothing divine about dealing with crap in your life. But then I did learn a few things.

I learnt to pay my own electricity bills, have the locks of the door opened when I forgot my keys inside the house (that happened quite a bit), and to get a new LPG cylinder. And, I even learnt how to get the telephone line fixed at home.

I had been struggling for days to get my telephone line moved to my new place, and it was just not happening. There are some things in India that simply don't work unless you 'grease palms'. Mathew, my colleague, suggested I try bribing the lineman. A real bribe to a stranger! I had never done it before. Though I always said it was against my principles, because it sounded so much cooler, the truth was that I was always scared I might have to go to jail if I got caught.

'No one sends you to jail for bribing a lineman,' Mathew told me.

I took a half day off from work, and headed straight to the telephone exchange. I told the receptionist I wanted to lodge a complaint because my phone line had not been installed for over a month. I showed her all the signs of being an angry young woman, who would bite off anyone's head who came in her way. So she took me seriously, and led me to a large room with a huge table and chairs on either side.

The man sitting at the table was on the phone. I waited for him to hang up. I was still unconvinced that I should bribe him.

The very idea of bribing was making me squirm. But I still kept the fifty-rupee note in my hand. This very well-spoken and well-mannered gentleman assured me that my phone would be fixed very soon.

'I need it done today, please. I cannot miss work every day like this,' I pleaded.

'Consider it done, Madam,' he said.

That was it. It was done indeed. I returned home and the phone line had been installed.

The next day there was excitement in the office.

'Excellent. How much did you give?' Mathew asked.

'You know, I was unsure if I should. I mean... the guy just looked so well-dressed and polished that somehow fifty bucks just seemed too little.'

'Well dressed? Who the hell did you go and see?'

'This person called Dhodbole. He had a large table, and even a nameplate with his name on it.'

Mathew looked up the phone directory, and started laughing.

'Good thing you didn't offer him the bribe because you would have definitely gone to jail.'

It turned out that he was the General Manager of the exchange, and not the linesman.

I felt a bit stupid, but also relieved that I had not gone against my sixth sense. How was I supposed to know? I had never been to a telephone exchange before that. I had no idea what a linesman looked like.

But if life is a teacher, I am a smart student.

～

I devoted myself to my work, and started doing things I had never dreamt I could do. It's funny how people think work is only about picking up your pay cheque at the end of the month. I was the youngest manager in the company. Work was fun. We were a small team: no politics or office gossip. Ah, okay, a little gossip, but nothing malicious. We fought about things we were passionate about, and it was all forgotten because, eventually, we all had the same goals. It was the same year that we organised the country's first CRS conference, and it instantly became the talk of the industry. Kamal told me how she had always wanted to do it, but never had a manager who could make it happen. I didn't stop smiling the entire month.

I started spending my free time on sports. All that love that I had developed for it as a fauji kid was paying off now. Though I couldn't improve my game of squash and I lost most of the time, it still left me with a sense of calmness that I was not able to find in yoga and meditation. Maybe it is a defect — to want action all the time, to not be able to enjoy the silence of the mind and the heart. But in a way, action was spiritual. The sweat-soaked t-shirt, the pain in the overworked muscles, the increased heart rate.

Every time I went out to play squash, the beginning was

tough. My mind had to tell my body to push itself. Soon I began to notice a pattern, that to get 'that *zen* feeling', all I had to do was hang in there. After a while, the body would enter a rhythm and the mind entered the blank zone, where I shut out everything — except following the ball moving back and forth between the racquets and the wall. There was a singular focus, just like others had in yoga. On the one hand, everything other than the ball was shut out of my mind, on the other hand, my thoughts were free to wander, to explore and challenge what I hadn't before. There was a tranquil existence mentally, supported by aggressive action physically — my kind of meditation! And that composure for half an hour everyday made my soul lighter.

It was not my imagination that I started to feel less angry and unhappy, I got into fewer arguments and the thought of forgiveness entered my mind. I started to think about a justification for what had happened beyond just the perspective of morality and value systems, beyond black and white. I realised that millions of things could have tipped the scales for such a thing to happen and most situations are difficult to judge from a right and wrong perspective. In the end, it was not about how or why, it was just the way it was.

The other thing I did a lot during those months was travel. Apart from other places that my work took me to, I went to Nepal four times. I suppose, like most Capricorns, I am a mountain goat at heart, and I had always wanted to see the Himalayas. I think the greatest inventors in the world were the Wright Brothers, speaking only of the relevance of inventions I am concerned with, never mind the carbon footprint.

The seed for the love of travel was sown in me when I was just five days old — when I took my very first driving vacation. By the time I was fifteen I had seen a whole lot of India, the diversity of which is so amazing. It is like countries within a country. It is true that travel is the greatest teacher.

I cannot pin my love of travel on one reason. Travelling gives different people different things. Some travel to find themselves, to meet people who are like them, and some to meet those unlike them. Some want to rediscover places where history was made.

Some to learn from different cultures, others to lose themselves to another world even if for a short period. Some want to share their experiences, while others want to create experiences. Some want to widen their horizons, others want to explore opportunities that are not possible unless they unleash that nomad within. Some travel to re-establish bonds, and some even travel to announce a newly-acquired status. Where you go, and how you travel, makes the ultimate statement about you after all. Whatever the reason the world travelled for, I travelled to heal my soul. The sound of the walkman playing songs from the *Sound of Music*, while I screeched along cacophonously ('These are a few of my favourite things'), in strange places, where no one knew me, left me smiling, happy and *peaceful*. Is there anything at all in the world comparable with what travelling does for the human spirit?

Chapter 39

My love for travel was something my mother would never understand. Every penny I spent on travel gave me joy ten times more than what I got buying that fridge and television. I am glad I didn't always listen to her, because I would never have had the incredible experiences and adventures I had travelling otherwise.

One such experience occurred when I was returning from one of my trips to Nepal. I was famished. I went to the restaurant and asked for a sandwich. It was about two dollars. I had less than that left in local currency. What I had was a hundred dollar bill. I took out all the change I had, and it still didn't add up to what I needed, so I decided to give the sandwich a miss.

A few minutes later, a man came up to me with the sandwich. He must have been around thirty. He had seen me at the restaurant counter and followed the drama as I ordered the sandwich, counted my money, returned the sandwich, and walked away.

Despite the time I had spent twiddling my thumbs at various airports, this sort of thing had never happened before.

Why had this stranger, whom I didn't even know (yes, I know that is what a stranger means, thank you) bought me a sandwich?

Maybe he wanted to chat me up. After all, we could be on the same flight. Maybe he knew I was from Bombay, and would now ask me for my address, dreaming about free accommodation. Maybe he wanted to marry an Indian girl and live in India forever. It was possible to imagine the wildest things, you know, now that I was single. Worse, maybe he was a drug peddler and wanted me to carry drugs for him. It was possible he had mixed something in the sandwich. Maybe he wanted to rob me! I was guilty of having entertained all those thoughts, but hey, it could happen to the best of us.

'I have the money, I just didn't want to change my dollars,' I explained.

'It's okay,' he said with a smile.

'Can I pay you back, please? You don't even know me!'

'It's okay. No need to pay money back.'

His English was not that good, and his accent confirmed he was German.

'When you see someone who need money, you remember me and you give. And one day, that person give to someone else. The world is round.'

I listened. I must admit I was a bit, just a very little bit, ashamed of myself, but I didn't let it show. I understood what he meant.

'Thank you.' I smiled.

He didn't stalk me, he didn't follow me to my house, and he didn't try to drug me. And so, a perfect stranger, whose name I will never know, taught me something.

Only after I returned home did I realise that I had taken such little notice of the world right under my nose. I was so wrapped up in my own life that I had not noticed how Lakshmi's life was different from mine. She had no privileges at all. No freedom. She lived every moment of her life the way others planned it for her, and she would never have any control over it.

And that is exactly how millions of girls like her are born, live, and die. In fact, she was one of the lucky ones to have survived because millions are killed at birth — only because they are girls.

Finally, her family found a boy willing to marry her. She wanted my sister and me to meet him. We went over to his place. The only thing that went in his favour was that his family was not asking for dowry. Her mother came over to discuss the wedding. I told her what I thought of him, which was not much.

'Didi, everyone wants land, cash, and gold. We don't have any. They only want to know what we can give her,' she said to me.

'And his family is not asking for anything?'

'They only want a grand wedding.'

'You barely have any money to eat, how will you give her a grand wedding?'

'I will take a loan. You can lend me some money, can't you?' she asked.

I was certainly in a better position than her, but hardly had pots of cash stashed away.

'How much will it cost you?'

'At least two lakhs.'

In my seven years of working I had not saved anything close to that figure!

'I don't have two lakhs,' I said honestly.

'Well, give me as much as you can. I will borrow from others, and from the money lender.'

'Do you know how much two lakhs is? You will be repaying loans all your life!'

'But at least he won't get himself drunk and beat her all the time.'

Surreal! Was I really having this conversation? They were just grateful that the guy was not going to beat her up! I don't think the discussion would have gone anywhere. Anyway, I belonged to another world. I thought about it, even more so now, because I had eaten a free sandwich at Kathmandu airport less than a month ago.

I asked myself if I could survive without the security of my savings. Then, I thought about all the years it had taken me to build that buffer and suddenly my perspective changed — for some reason, it looked like an interesting challenge: I wondered how long it would take me to earn what I had saved so far considering I earned more than I had ever earned in the past seven years? A couple of years *at best* I figured!

I went to the bank and cleaned out my savings. Though I gave her the money telling her I expected it back, so that she would value it, I knew in my heart that it would never come back. I am not telling you this to make myself look good, though I can imagine it does make me look a little nice, but you must know that giving without any expectation of return, to someone who was not my blood, was very liberating. The detachment from material possessions is a kind of freedom you cannot experience unless you give it all away — at least once in a lifetime. I had done it for myself.

And so Lakshmi was married.

Every day when I went to work in the crowded city of Bombay, I saw thousands of people striving to make their lives better — fathers trying to earn extra money so that the children could be sent to 'English speaking schools'; mothers who woke before sunrise to cook the meals for their children, and then set out to work themselves; small children trying to sell you something so that they could buy a meal. Every morning, from the balcony of my apartment I saw an old man recovering from a stroke, trying to walk holding his walker, one step at a time. The eight-year-old boy who lived next door took insulin injections before he went out to play.

They were all heroes — nameless and faceless to the world, dealing with their difficult circumstances every day, and living with the hope that one day their life would get better. No one would ever know who they were. Unlike Sudha Chandran, the dancer who returned to performing after losing her leg in an accident, or Lisa Ray who beat cancer and then went on to helping others who were fighting the disease, their struggles and stories would never be known, yet, they fought the good fight every day. They still tried.

After a point, Lakshmi's life and mine moved in different directions. I will never know if she was beaten by a drunk husband, or if she managed to give her children a better life, and of course, I never saw the money.

Chapter 40

After completing five of the six semesters in college, and having spent a good chunk of Suraj's hard-earned money and my own, I dropped out. In the absence of any other justifiable excuse, I like to blame my break-up with Zaid for that. It was to be my very last semester, just a few more months, but I stopped going to college and I never got that degree. Maybe I was just bored.

Now I was officially single, broke, and a college dropout! It felt awesome — because there comes a point in your life when things are so bad that they can't get worse.

You got anything else for me? Just bring it on! I said to God.

It wasn't just that. It was also as if bit by bit, I was wiping things away from my cluttered slate of life, cutting off from attachments — perhaps towards a natural progression into a new life. My sheer existence seemed a bit lighter. I spent a lot of time with my friends, but something had changed between Nicky and me over the years.

Shiv lived close to my new place, and that was why we ended up spending a lot more time with each other. I liked most things about him except his bratty teenage girlfriend. I would always give him a hard time about her, and he would tell me to shut up.

Shiv's mother had died of cancer two years before, and his father was suffering from Lou Gehrig's disease. Yes, even I had never heard of it until I met him. In layman's terms, it is a motor neuron disease. He was inching towards death, slowly losing all control over his nervous system. But he was a spirited man. By the time Shiv and I met, he had already lost control over his limbs, and was confined to a wheelchair, but his personality shone through. He would crack jokes and behave as if nothing in his life had changed. I loved his zing for life.

'It must be very difficult for all of you to be normal with him,' I said to Shiv.

I think he found my question stupid.

'Everything is normal, and he is not afraid of dying. He says it's not how you die, but how you live that matters.'

'Do you talk to him about death?'

'He talks to us about it. He wants us to understand it, so that we can deal with it when the time comes.'

'Understand what?' I was always willing to get drawn into a discussion about death.

'That death is not the end; it is just a continuation of the journey. Living forever is not the agenda. He says that it is true that to go to heaven you have to die.'

'But no one knows what will happen. There is no evidence that the soul exists.'

'It's the same as *knowing* God exists — even though you don't really know it. He exists because you believe he does. In the end it's all about faith.'

I was thinking of a counter argument, but Shiv beat me to it.

'Yes, there is no evidence that death is not the end but just another beginning. There's no evidence that the soul exists, but you don't know for sure that death is really the end either... do you?'

He had got me there because that was not something I could argue with, at least not until I died myself — and by then it would be too late to offer any theories to the living world. I wondered how death must feel — even if it was ultimately the end of all feelings.

God must have thought, *Do you really want the answers? Lemme help you.*

I made one of my trips to Nepal with Mathew and Sara, my

friends at work. During that vacation we hitchhiked stopping trucks and lorries on the way, something I would never do without a boy with me. So, yes, there are some things only boys can do, just like my mother said! We drove through Chitwan National Park one night, and a pair of tiger cubs crossed our path. We went mountain biking, and I saw the Himalayas. It was all wonderful until we went river rafting.

The sun was blazing that morning and, by noon, my head had started throbbing. I started to relax a bit instead of paddling to control the raft. As we went through one of the rough rapids, the raft flew into the air. If I had had one foot fixed under the folds of the raft, as I was supposed to, I would have been fine, but I had just let my guard down seconds before that.

At first I was tossed up like a pancake, and then plunged down into the ice-cold water. I had lost my focus for a split second, and it had taken just that much time for the accident to happen. Although I had the life jacket on, I couldn't reach the surface because the raft was on top on me.

It was dark. In my desperation I thought of Sameer, Maria's boyfriend, who had also drowned. I was not ready to die yet, no matter how baked or half-baked my theories on death were. I had a single thought in my head — *I must get out.*

The rays of the sun were shining above the edges of the raft.

My thoughts then turned to my friends, Mathew and Sara. I thought of what they would go through trying to carry a dead body in a coffin across international boundaries. Oh, the paperwork! I had worked for an airline, and I knew what a pain it was!

I cannot allow myself to die. God, not now! I called my hotline.

And, of course, magically, I moved slower than the raft and, after sometime, came up. I saw a rescue team — one man in a canoe to be precise. He was nothing like the smashing hero who comes out of nowhere and rescues the lead female character in the movies, but I did not complain. I am a reasonable person most of the time. Anyway, he ferried me to the other end, where the raft and my friends were waiting for me.

I could have died that day. I had not just lost concentration on the raft that morning; it was as though I had lost focus on what I wanted from life. We all get what we want from life, but for the Laws of Attraction to work, I first needed to know what I wanted. This was why God had put me through this experience. If I had died there that night — that would have been it. A boring albeit dramatic climax! I took stock of my life with the stars twinkling above, and the Himalayas as the backdrop, as if they were witnesses to my 'bucket list'.

I wanted to find love. I wanted to have children. I wanted to travel, and I wanted to always be fit and healthy.

Chapter 41

That was how I understood that I could live without a man, but I wanted to live with one. I had a single point programme now — not to remain single. It was the purpose of finding love (that was an alternative title for this book for a long time).

And thus started the search for a new man. My sister was my most passionate matchmaker. Ever since she had returned from the US, there was not a single man she knew who had not been evaluated for me as a prospective boyfriend. Right from her office colleagues to her college friends, her associates at work, and even customers, suppliers, vendors, and friends' friends. Just about any man who was single would immediately be put under my sister's scanner. She even suggested to a guy that his girlfriend was not good enough and so he should consider me instead.

She was direct and committed. Her opening introduction line to every single man became, 'She is single, and so are you.'

It was very embarrassing, but I went out on quite a few dates. So many that it became a joke. Every morning as soon as I got to work, the others said 'Good Morning' to each other, but Mathew and Sara greeted me with, 'Who paid the bill?'

They knew a secret that I am about to share with you.

Going on all these dates was fine, but whenever it came to paying the bill, I didn't know how to handle it. How does one decide what to do with the bill when the person you date is not someone you know? Usually, it was okay to let the guy pay, but I felt obliged in a way. At times I would end up dating some really idiotic men, and I didn't want to feel obliged to them. Some men found it difficult to deal with girls who wanted to split the bill or pay it themselves. So this was really the part that was hard to get right.

I invented my own rules. If I didn't like a guy I went out with, I would pay the bill; and if I liked him, he could pay. More than the act, it was the philosophy behind it I enjoyed. I was a princess, and it was an honour — a privilege — for him to take me out. And, if I never wanted to see the guy again, I grabbed the bill to settle it, and ran for my life. I didn't care what he thought because I was never going to see him again anyway! Occasionally, I met guys who were not really my sort of men, but we would strike a friendship. At times like this I was happy to go Dutch.

Mathew and Sara were very amused, and I had been paying quite a few bills!

'At this rate you will have a hand-to-mouth existence very soon,' said Sara. 'You should review your rules because they are very bad financial decisions.'

I was the butt of their jokes. And so the saga of my dating went on. Completely celibate dating, I have to add reluctantly. I made that choice only because I wanted to be focused. I was not going to get distracted by casual sex, and I was not looking for a short term 'let's-get-to-know-each-other-and-we-will-go-with-the-flow' kind of crap. It had to be the whole nine yards or nothing. No wishy-washy. I didn't want to waste my time.

One of my sister's colleagues, Anjana, was getting married. She had met her man on the Internet. The Internet had changed the world. Websites were cropping up, and email had made it easy for people to communicate with each other from any corner of the world. You were not restricted to dating people in your college campus or at your workplace.

My sister was not going to leave this option unexplored.

'That's it — you need to get on the Internet.'

She created a Hotmail account for me, my first personal email account. Then she set up my profile on one of the singles sites. It was a sweet introduction, but much like a matrimonial column a child would write for her mother.

My Internet explorations took me to rediff.com. Those days their marketing slogan was 'You can find anything on rediff. com' — and I thought I must take their word for it. I went ahead and registered on their singles site. I had to specify what sort of relationship I was looking for, that is, choose from: men looking for men, men looking for women, women looking for men. Then I had to choose if I was looking for a long-term or short-term relationship, friends, dating, partying, and the like. And I had to write a short note about myself.

As I got down to writing it, an amazing fact struck me. After all the time I had spent on the planet trying to make my mark, I could actually capture it all in less than half a page. It was very dissatisfying (another reason why I really had to write this book). Anyway, going back to the story, my introduction specifically stated that I had been married before, and that I was looking for a long-term relationship.

I could not put my finger on what exactly I was looking for in a man. I could not say I wanted to be with someone who had such and such education, or such and such financial background, who was this tall or this fat, from this or that city, so and so religion, born on this date, month, or year. I did not have any of those pre-requisites. Some people do need to know those things about prospective spouses, but I was not looking for any of that. I wanted only one thing — magic!

And in my enthusiasm I added that if I found it, I would change my life for it — even if it meant moving to hell!

Chapter 42

It is unbelievable how many lonely hearts there are out there. God bless the Internet, and God bless all modes of communication that allow people to find each other!

I started getting a lot of emails. I would receive about twenty-five to thirty emails a day, of which I would find only about seven or eight worth replying to. Out of those, about two to three would actually go beyond one exchange with the author, and about one a day would end in a correspondence that lasted for over a week.

I did that for two to three months. So you can do the math. It was more complicated and time consuming than applying for a job. Whoever said love comes easy?

After virtual chit-chat there was another level. I exchanged phone numbers with half of the men with whom I had corresponded for over a week; and from the people I had spoken to, I met half. That would be, what the world calls 'blind dating'.

Some were just taking a chance — to see if I would be available for a one night stand. I came across men who were half my size and three-quarters my age, and looked like my sons when I met them. Some invited me to the seediest and creepiest restaurants I had to escape from. I came across doctors, engineers, a pilot, an American wedding photographer, bankers, auctioneers, a scrap-ship seller, software engineers, more software engineers, managers of corporations, an Australian deep sea diver, musicians, a hotelier, a leather manufacturer, and even a horse trainer from

France who could write only in French (that I couldn't speak at all)! I could easily have compiled a bestseller about various career options.

Emails poured in from all corners of India, the UK, US, the Middle East, and Australia. It was a broad bandwidth and I was multi-tasking.

One of the men I came across through the Internet was Dev. He was based in Seattle. We exchanged emails once every few days. He was an Aries. Though he was from Chennai, he had been in the US for over twelve years. Of course, since he was there and I was exactly at the other end of the planet, meeting was not the easiest thing to arrange, but we corresponded often and even spoke frequently.

Another was Alex. We had spoken a few times. He played the violin, had done his MBA, and was working with an advertising agency. He sounded incredibly sexy. In fact, I was worried that he would think I didn't look like Cindy Crawford! We agreed to have lunch at Jazz by the Bay. He called me that morning to tell me we could meet at one o' clock. He said he would be in a pink shirt and black trousers.

'What kinda guy wears a pink shirt?' I asked Mathew.

I arrived on time, and took a table facing the entrance so that I could spot my blind date. Blue shirt — no, not the one. White shirt — no. Pin stripes — no. Ten minutes later came pink. My heart sank when I saw him. It wasn't even a soft pink that's usually close to white. It was PINK — like the colour of my fake nose when I acted as a clown in school. And he wore a tie with purple and orange orchids on it! It looked like a souvenir from the Thailand Tourism Board. And the looks? They didn't match the voice one bit. Personality? It couldn't be this guy's. He came up to my table because I was the only woman sitting alone.

'Are you Gauri?'

'Sorry, not me. I was just leaving.' I couldn't even smile.

Of course I was hardly a Miss Universe myself to look for a potential Gladrags cover model, a hot hunk or trophy husband, but with my loud voice and ability to attract wanted and unwanted attention, it was unlikely I would go unnoticed in a roomful of people. I needed someone whose personality I would not overpower. After that I became smart, and started asking for photographs if I had the slightest interest in a guy.

'That was a quick lunch,' Mathew teased me.

'Yup, I wasn't in the mood to pay any bills today,' I laughed.

Another time, five minutes after meeting my date I figured there was no way I could spend an hour and a half having lunch with him. I escaped the punishment of having to suffer his company for an entire meal by disappearing from the back door on the pretext of going to the washroom. But what took the cake was that Rima and I once ended up dating the same guy! Yes, through Rediff's Members of the Lonely Heart Club!

But let's be honest, there were a couple of guys I had liked too, but it didn't go anywhere. There was no magic. At best I got entertainment and an education. At the end of that period I could tell at a glance how things would turn out to be, and my assessments were bang on target.

Then suddenly it stopped being fun. I was broke paying restaurant bills, emotionally drained, physically tired, and disappointed. I stopped checking my mails. I logged on only when my inbox was full.

By September, I was so down and out that if there was a Miss Feeling-Bad-For-Yourself contest, I would have won hands down. The rushed life of Bombay, a city that had always given me hope, got on my nerves. The job that I so loved — seemed like a money-trap. The things I had collected in my home felt like a burden. I felt a desperate urge to flee from my surroundings. I needed a break. But I was completely broke.

Sometime then, Zaid and I met for coffee. He had said that he wanted to give me something. It was a letter — addressed to my parents. Though it was addressed to them, I suspect that he had left it unsealed because he wanted me to read it and since I would have read it anyway, I decided to read it in front of him.

Without explaining his actions, he had apologised for causing turmoil in everyone's life. He thanked them for having accepted him (despite his unmatched religious status) and said that he was sorry for what he had done. I quietly folded the letter and put it back in the envelope. Then out of the blue, without thinking and for no related reason at all I said, 'I need some money!'

There was a pause. I waited for him to ask me why I wanted it, but he didn't.

'How much do you need?'

'I want to go to the US.' I was asking him to pay for the trip. Not a penny more, not a penny less.

I have no idea what went through his mind. Maybe he was smiling at the thought of finding a weak-spot in the armour of the super-independent woman, the one with the inflated ego having to borrow money — and it wasn't even for something most people consider necessary! I could have deferred the trip.

Maybe I could have also borrowed from someone else! But, without exchanging a word between us, I had offered him the explanation by asking for the money, immediately after reading the letter. Though it was not pre-meditated, that was exactly the reason I was asking him for the money — I had come up with a wonderful opportunity to offer him *redemption*.

Zaid and I had filed for divorce by mutual consent. I had not taken any alimony. Maybe if I had not been earning, it would have been a different situation, but it would have also been a different life. And yet, a part of me wanted to make him pay for what he had done one way or the other.

'I will arrange it,' he said without hesitation. Perfect. He literally got to 'pay' for his mistakes, and I got to go on a vacation and though I never passed on that letter to my parents, in the end we both got what we wanted.

I made my itinerary: Los Angeles, where I would see my sister's boyfriend; Chicago — because I always wanted to go to the city of Jazz; Cincinnati — where Anjana (who had found her husband on the Internet) now lived; New York — to visit Zaid's sister; and finally Washington DC, where I would have the finale of a grand American vacation.

I told Dev about my trip, and he invited me to Seattle. I was hesitant. I didn't want to go to his 'territory'. I gave him my itinerary, and told him he could meet me anywhere he liked, but I would not visit his city.

'I am on a vacation, particularly from dating,' I told Shiv who, like Sara and Mathew, had a real interest in my love life.

'I will bet my sweet ass that you will not be single when you return.'

This time I didn't care about what my mother had to say about my trip. The day before I was leaving, Rima came over.

We went to the salon. Amongst other things, I chopped my long locks and permed my hair. Then we spent the evening at home packing for my trip.

As we sat chatting after dinner, we started reminiscing about the old days. She told my sister the story of how I had become her roommate.

'Will anyone believe that's the girl who came crying to my room ten years ago?' She laughed. Technically, she was laughing at me, but I noticed a sense of pride in her voice. Ten years had gone by, and she had played her part in making me what I had become.

Ten years. I had wanted to leave my home — I did, and I even made a decent life. I had discovered a whole new world, an amazing one — an imperfect place where living was not always about winning, and where people and relationships changed constantly. I had thought life should be black and white, but now I knew there were greys — and a lot of other amazing colours. I had learnt my lessons and they were different from everyone else's; acquired my own *wisdom* — that was more valuable than the *knowledge* I had gained in school. I had learnt to accept life as it is — with all its ups and downs. Yes, I had learnt that while I could rarely control my circumstances, how I dealt with them was up to me. I was in charge of my own destiny, and I had every reason to be proud of myself.

In ten years I had discovered that in this world with billions of people, I was unique just like my DNA, and it was perfectly okay. I had experienced the joy of detachment and I had learnt to take from life. I had hated living alone, but now I knew that I could do it. The girl sitting here this evening was not an insecure child craving emotional comfort.

'Now she makes other people cry,' my sister joked.

It was listening to the two of them speak about me that I realised that the love and acceptance I had been seeking since childhood — *had always been there*. For a fleeting moment I thought about all the people in my life. Yes, I was loved. And adored.

I accused Rima of taking advantage of the fact that I didn't know any stories of her geeky days. We talked about Riya and Asha. Both of them were married, as my parents would say — 'settled'. But Rima was still single. A couple of times she had come close to committing herself, but she hadn't.

'Don't you want to get married?' my sister asked her.

'It's not such a big deal. If it happens, fine... but if it doesn't, I don't care. I will probably be happy just adopting a child and raising her all by myself,' she replied. Her family would have accepted that and honestly, what is the big deal about being single forever?

It was six in the morning, and the sun came out. If I didn't have to go to the airport, we would have continued chatting — shredding Dermont Mulroney to pieces for being the worst part of *My Best Friend's Wedding*, making a list of all the places we wanted to visit together, planning a reunion on our twentieth 'meeting anniversary', and condemning liposuction — thinking we would never get *that* fat anyway.

As we were driving to the airport, it started drizzling. I was staring out of the window with a blank mind when we crossed a man on a bicycle. His pillion rider was a little girl in a uniform with a school bag. His clothes were shabby and torn, and hers dirty. The drizzle was turning to rain but they didn't run for shelter. They were enjoying the rain, singing loudly, the little girl's arms extended — trying to catch the raindrops as if each came with a measure of happiness. It was not an ordinary sight. I felt a glow, as if God was talking to me, telling me that no matter what my circumstances were, I was responsible for my happiness.

Rima and my sister saw me off. The plane took off and I felt like a brand new person; it was not just because of my hairdo.

Chapter 43

I landed in LA on a lovely October morning. My sister's boy-friend picked me up, and together we did all the things tourists do there. We took pictures in front of the Hollywood sign, went skating on Venice Beach, drove past Beverly Hills, pretended to shop at Rodeo Drive, and checked out the Walk of Fame.

I imagined how one day, soon after he completed his studies, my sister would get married to him removing her physical presence from my life... but it was okay. I had lived my life exactly as I pleased, and she had the right to do the same.

One night while he and I were fast asleep, there was an earthquake. In a matter of minutes the entire neighbourhood was on the streets. With my encounter with LA thus truly complete, I moved on to Chicago. Chicago was great. I loved everything about the city. Shiv's childhood friend lived there, and he was very hospitable. He showed me around whenever he had the time. When he was not free, I went on my own expeditions. I took the hop-on/hop-off bus tour. I love those in every damn city I visit. I spent an entire day at the fine arts museum, and an evening in a jazz bar. I went alone on all the rides on the Navy Pier and finally, I saw the world from the top of the Sears Tower.

I had never been on any building that had over a hundred floors. It was a windy day, and I could feel the building sway. I have to be honest — I didn't even have the guts to look down, but I couldn't wipe the smile off my face once I was up there. There is an entire movie on the story behind the Sears Tower, and over a million people visit this nearly forty-year-old building each year.

Meanwhile, Dev happened to be in India that week for work. I checked my email from time to time to keep in touch with my sister. While I was in Chicago, I received an email from Mathew. He had forwarded something that had been circulated to all employees that morning. An industry giant had acquired a majority stake in our company, in line with their global strategy to expand their distribution in the Asia-Pacific region. I thought of Kamal, who would probably be most affected by this because the new company would bring in their own managers. So, some high-level continent-wide-acquisition decision that we had no control over was going to steer her career now.

This was on my mind when I landed in Cincinnati. I stayed with Anjana. She was 'just-married' and she had not yet found a job because Cincinnati was... well, Cincinnati — a small town with few opportunities and even fewer things to see and do! So we spent most of our time 'bonding'.

Her husband and she took me out to a lovely restaurant and, one evening over dinner, they told me about Viren.

Everybody was just trying to do their bit to help me find a man.

'You know, I am just up to my ears with this dating bit. This is supposed to be my break-from-the-boys-trip.'

'Okay, don't think of him as a date. Just go out for dinner with him. He's awesome fun; I know you will like him.'

So I agreed to dinner the following evening.

In the morning Anjana and I went to the library because she had to return a book. I was not allowed inside because I was not a member, so she suggested that I check my email at the facility area just outside while I waited for her. I thought my sister might have dropped me a line.

I logged on, but there was no email from my sister. In fact there was only one email — from Rediff. Since I had twenty minutes and nothing to do, I went against my self-imposed ban and read it. It was from a guy called Uday. He had spent parts of his life in Australia as a student of fine arts, in the UK looking after mentally challenged children, in Bosnia as a UN Volunteer, and in New York with his uncle, before returning to Chennai. He broke up with his wife of five years, some time ago.

Now, remember I had twenty minutes and nothing to do. I was 'off' men, and had no intention of taking this to any level.

When you are gambling on the tables of Vegas, the way you behave when you have little at stake is very different from how you behave when you have a lot at stake.

That was the reason why my response to Uday was curt, and even a little rude. I wrote:

Hey,

Nice introduction! Is this something you write to all prospective brides to impress them? Well, I am not looking for a short-term relationship. And, even if it scares you, I want marriage and my own kids — you know, the biological clock is ticking away and all that... So let's not waste each other's time if we don't want the same things.

And, by the way, I need a photo. No photo, no further discussion.

Gauri

It was a bit intimidating, I thought. *Maybe I should change something? Well, it is what it is. Let him deal with it!* But, on an impulse, I added a postscript: *Being Indian, I hope you know Gauri means bright. It is the brilliant golden sunlight that shines upon the mountains as the sun rises.*

And after that I got down to writing a long email to my sister.

That was the night I was supposed to have dinner with Viren. He was not supposed to be a date, so I don't know why I changed five times before I settled for the jeans and sweatshirt I wore. He came over to pick me up, and was exactly as Anjana had described him. As soon as I saw him, I decided this would be a date. I wanted to change again, but that would have made me look very dumb, so I quickly painted my face a bit. And that was how I headed out with my eyeliner all smudged. He too was Aries. And though he had cooked us a vegetarian meal because he was Tambram, it was an awesome evening. I even pretended to love vegetarian food! I couldn't remember the last time I had had so much fun. Just before dinner I went to the loo, and that was when I saw myself in the mirror. Oh God! I returned to the table with no eyeliner.

At some point after dinner, we started looking at his photos on his computer. I asked him if I could check my email. It would be morning in India, and I was sure my sister Nandini would have replied to me. When I logged on, there were two emails in my inbox — one from my sister and one from Uday. I was surprised. I hadn't thought he would respond.

He had sent me a picture. I showed it to Viren.

'What do you think?'

'I think he looks like a hippy.'

He did look like a hippy. His long, curly locks that ran all the way to his shoulders were tied in a ponytail. He wore glasses — like John Lennon — with round frames that hid his large eyes, and he had a bright smile! In the photo he was in the centre with two people on either side, and his long arms were wrapped around them. 'Let's see what he has written,' I said. And so Viren and I read Uday's reply together.

Dear Gauri,

Why is a twenty-seven-year young woman worried about the biological clock ticking away?

Well, this is sort of the best introduction I could cook up for the thirty-three years of my life. I am glad you liked it because it is difficult to impress people in the first email.

Your introduction says you are looking for magic, and would be willing to move to hell if you found it. So where in heaven do you live right now?

I am sending you a picture, and I look forward to seeing one of yours.

Uday

P.S – Brilliant golden sunlight that shines upon the mountains as the sun rises.... The meaning of Uday, you may know, is sunrise!

I was immediately embarrassed about my first email. I had been anticipating a reaction, because that is what I give to people, but he had sent me a response. I softened my tone in my reply — with a little help from my date for the evening. And I sent him a picture.

He too was an Aries. Now, just when I had decided to take a complete break from men and dating, I had three of them — all south Indian, and all three Aries!

Chapter 44

Viren was a ladies' man. He drove me to the airport the next morning. As I kissed him goodbye, we exchanged our watches as mementos of a great date. I loved big-dial wristwatches. And only because I wanted to lay my hands on his very funky, style-statement watch, I had offered him mine (so that he would offer me his).

Zaid's sister picked me up at New York, and I stayed with her. She was a working woman, so I had the freedom to choose how I spent my mornings. I chose to spend them writing emails all day. After all, now I had three men to write to.

Uday's sister lived in Pittsburgh, close to Washington DC, and he encouraged me to go and see her. I called her, and we had a cordial chat. Like me, he too had a brother and a sister, and his sister's name was exactly the same as my sister's!

But missing a tour of Washington DC just because our sisters had the same name would have been a bit much. That was when I told him about Dev. After all, Dev had been in the picture for weeks, and we had finally decided to meet up. Also, I did want to see DC, so I decided to stick to my original plan.

And so now Uday knew Dev existed, but Dev did not know Uday existed, and Zaid's sister, who was still technically my sister-in-law because the divorce would take another couple of months to come through, knew that all three men — Dev, Uday and Viren — existed in my life! She asked me to show her their pictures.

'He looks c-u-t-e,' she said looking at Viren's photograph — one that I had taken at his house. *What the heck, he was good-looking!*

'So what do you think about him?' I showed her Dev's picture.

'He looks young!' Despite being ten years older than me, Dev didn't look a day over thirty.

'He lives in Seattle.' I told her.

And finally she saw Uday's picture.

'He looks like someone who is very good at giving hugs,' she said thoughtfully.

Ah, that. Physical contact! Great sex equals great marriage? Somewhat true, I guess — especially if you intend to spend the rest of your life in a monogamous relationship. But I am greedy for those hugs and cuddles as well.

'Who do you like?' she asked.

'Hmm, I haven't even met Dev and Uday yet.'

As the conversation progressed, she realised that I was serious about moving on with my life.

'You will stop being my sister-in-law in a few months,' she said. There was sadness in her eyes.

'But I will always be your sister, and that is better than being a sister-in-law,' I tried to lighten the situation.

You can try as much as you want to make the moment less painful, but saying goodbye is never easy. I was going to leave New York the next day. I did not know if I would ever see her again. Even if I did, the next time we would meet, she would not be my sister-in-law.

There was something else too. This was my chance to bring it up. When Zaid and I married — for public consumption that is — his mother had given me some jewellery. She had told me it had been passed down to her from her in-laws. It was a family heirloom. As the daughter-in-law of the house, I had become the new owner.

'About the jewellery — I want you to keep it, and give it to whoever Zaid marries next,' I said to her.

She started crying. 'Please don't do this. She gave it to you, and it is yours. She is gone, and it would make her very unhappy.'

'She gave it to me as Zaid's wife, and I am not his wife any more. I would really like it to stay in the family.'

She knew what I meant, but her conscience would not allow her to accept it. It was a very unhappy moment for both of us. We both knew that the future was about to change forever.

'He is my brother and I love him; I will eventually have to accept his decisions and his choices.'

'I know, and that is the right thing for you to do as his sister — to support him.'

Sometime during the months that had gone by, I had forgiven Zaid. I wasn't angry with him any longer. Unlike Suraj, I didn't have any feelings for Zaid. He was just another person to me now. I had even tried to justify his relationship with Maria to myself. Maybe it was something that had just happened, something that they had no control over — love can be like that. Maybe we had lost the togetherness. Maybe there had never been enough intensity in our relationship to last a lifetime in the first place.

'Are you going to sit here day and night sending emails? Don't you want to see New York?'

Finally, she said that she would not allow me to go back unless I had seen the Statue of Liberty. So we went to see the monument dedicated to freedom and a new life. How much more symbolic could it get? She took me to Macy's, and bought me my very first *Guess* watch. We went up the Twin Towers. No one could have imagined at that point that they would cease to be a part of the New York skyline in less than two years. She also took me to the very first musical treat at Broadway. We watched *Cats,* Broadway's longest running musical and, though she hated cats in real life, she suffered a musical about them just to entertain me. And thus, in one day, I saw everything people came to New York for.

She saw me off at the airport the next day. I called her as soon as I landed at DC, and told her where she could find the jewellery I wanted to return. I had hidden it in her house, and now that I was never going to see her again, she had no choice but to keep it.

'Sometimes, you are so stubborn Gauri, that you would put a donkey to shame,' she said. I smiled to myself. There was some truth in that.

Chapter 45

At Washington DC, my friend Siddhart and his Japanese girlfriend picked me up at the airport. They were both students, and lived in a cosy little studio apartment. I stayed with them for three days. Dev arrived the same evening. It was late. Even though he had been on a plane for over five hours from Seattle, he was ready to paint the town red. I, on the other hand, had no idea he would expect me to go out partying with him right away. I had assumed he would go to the hotel that evening, and we would meet the next morning. We had talked about exploring Washington DC together since neither of us had been there before.

So the first time he and I met, I was in my pyjamas, ready to hit the sack. He had hired the most expensive red convertible. A total waste on a person like me — because I didn't even recognise a sports car in the first place!

'I am sorry, I was ready for bed. I didn't know you wanted to go out.'

I offered to get dressed. I think he was a bit mad because he felt he had flown from one end of the US to the other just to meet me, and here I was greeting him in my pyjamas, not even some reasonably sexy nightwear!

But he tried to diffuse the tension, and decided to go to the hotel, calling it a night. We fixed on meeting for breakfast the next morning. Siddhart was definitely not impressed with him.

'I don't think your friends like me,' Dev said the next morning at breakfast.

'They don't have to like you.'

Why is the whole world running in a popularity contest? My brain babbled all the time.

After that I tried hard to be nice to him. He and I spoke about our past lives, as we hopped from one museum to another. Dev was a little fiery and had varied interests. But our meeting was a bit like a job interview. I knew he was asking me questions to judge me, and I said all the things he wanted to hear. How did it matter?

The day passed peacefully. After our tour of DC, he offered to take me to dinner at a romantic (and expensive) Italian restaurant.

Now, let me ask, do I remotely sound like a girl who would appreciate a candle-lit dinner where she cannot see what she is eating? The brightest spot at this dinner was the cute Italian bartender! Dev ordered the fanciest sounding wine on the wine list, which, again, was wasted on a person like me because, beyond the colour of the wine, I did not know the difference between wine from California and Australia.

And, suddenly, over this silly wine, we had an argument. He made a comment about the drinking habits of Indians. Oh my God! He had forgotten I was every bit a patriotic fauji kid!

'Look at you. You left the country more than ten years ago for greener pastures. It was just money. You make no economic contribution to the country, and you are sitting here passing judgments on Indians! Go back home, look into the mirror, and ask yourself how much more Indian you can get!'

Ouch.

I asked for the bill and paid it. It was a bloody hundred dollars!

I had joked to Dev about my principle of paying dating bills, but I had no reason to believe that I would ever have to do that with him.

He was very upset. He begged that I allow him to pay the bill, even if I did not like him at that moment, but I was adamant. I am not sure if it was because I was a bit tipsy, or because I didn't care. I think I was just enjoying making him look bad, and I continued to treat him badly. Just as he was driving me home — yes, in this fancy red convertible, something else came over me. I had

Internet access at Siddhart's place, but I asked Dev to take me to an Internet café.

I logged on to my email account and pulled out the picture of a man.

'Here, see this guy? I am marrying him,' I said.

'I don't like how he looks,' he said.

'It is not you, but I who has to like how he looks, because it is not you but me who's marrying him.'

Yeah, get that dude? My grey cells were babbling again.

He dropped me back to Siddhart's place. He was sure it was a joke I had made up to make him feel worse. He was to pick me up at nine the next morning to continue our DC tour. At six-thirty the phone rang.

'Hi Gauri, this is Dev.'

I hadn't been that drunk the previous night, but that early in the morning, half asleep, I had forgotten about where I was and what had happened.

'Hey, what's up?'

'I just called to tell you that I am going back to Seattle. I mean, right now. I am calling you from the airport.'

'What happened?'

There was a pause. Oh my God, it was not a question, I had opened the floodgates!

'What happened? You are asking me *what happened?* Ha, that's funny. Let me tell you what happened. I hate flying, Gauri. I was in India for work last week, where I was working eighteen hours a day! On Thursday I sat on a plane for twenty-two hours to get home. The basement of my house was flooded. I spent the entire day clearing it out so that I could sit on another plane for five hours to come and see you. And then... *you* happened. *Do you understand that? Do you have any idea what it means?* I am sorry, but I just can't deal with *you!*'

Now I was wide awake. 'I am sorry you feel this way,' I said, but I was not sorry. I was smiling. It was not even a smile, it was an evil grin. His comment on the drinking habits of Indians was in fact a great chance for me to make an 'exit of honour'. Why? Because I knew something he didn't know.

Chapter 46

I was in love. Since I had reached New York, a crazy exchange of emails had started. Flirting had come to a point where we were discussing the names of our children and pet dogs!

This was quite safe because if one person backed out, it could always be called a joke, and it could also mean something if you wanted it to. We were behaving as if we had already had an imaginary marriage. Two days before I had met Dev, it was Diwali.

What would you like for Diwali, sweetheart? Said an email.

Maybe you could ask me a QUESTION?

Do I make your heart go boing?

That is not the question I want you to ask me.

That is not the answer to my question.

Yes, the cat and mouse game. But the suspense of where this would go was very hard to deal with. I sat on the edge of my chair for days, as if I was watching the climax scene of a thriller. *What will happen next?*

I *had* to do something. I am a girl who likes to take what she wants, and so, one fine day I slipped in an email between our criss-crossing emails. The email had nothing in the body. It had only two words in the subject line: MARRY ME.

And this was how I proposed to a man, for the first time in my life, two days before I was going to meet Dev — on a date planned weeks ago.

He replied to every email I sent him, except this one. We had, however, started discussing a venue for our wedding.

I returned to Bombay that Saturday. Nandini was waiting for me at home. And, like Shiv had predicted, I was not single when I returned. It had all happened so quickly that it was very difficult to explain what was going on. The news spread like wildfire. Shiv came over to see me at home.

'I knew you were going to get yourself hooked to a guy in the US.'

'He's not from the US, he's from Chennai.'

'Chennai? How the hell did you meet him in the US?'

'I haven't met him yet.'

'Are you crazy? Look at your life. You are getting married to a guy you have never even met?'

'That is exactly the reason I am marrying him. His name is Uday.'

'You don't know him at all, Gauri!' he said seriously.

'Zaid and I had lived with each other for over two years, and it turned out that I didn't know *him* at all. Trust me, Uday is just perfect.'

'What does he do?'

'He manages a family business.'

'Family business? Even a guy who sells eggs at the corner of the street has a family business! Does he earn enough?'

'What is enough?'

I had no clue about how much he earned. Honestly. All I knew was that he lived alone in a rented house in Chennai, but we had not had this discussion because I was free from the bond of financial dependence.

Shiv was asking me the obvious questions any sensible person would ask in a normal situation. But this was not a normal situation, and therefore there could not be any normal answers.

'Okay, so you can support yourself. But what about your job? What about your life here?'

'What about it? I will get another job. I started from a scratch when I came here, and I made something of myself. I can do it again.'

'It is a big risk, Gauri. You are playing with your life.'

Ah, RISK. Finally. Now he was talking sense. True, I was taking a big risk. And he was rightly concerned about my madness. After all he, like my sister, cared about what happened to me. Risk is usually a chance that something might go wrong. And guess what is on the other side of the coin?

'It is, but no risk, no gain. I know it looks like a very impulsive decision but trust me, it is not. I know this is the magic I was waiting for.'

Over the years, many of my friends have told me that I was insane, as well as fortunate that Uday didn't turn out to be a serial killer, or even a woman pretending to be a man! That is why I had to write this story. That is exactly the point.

That is why I had to start from the beginning — because where I was going was the result of where I had come from. What use was experience if it had taught me nothing?

Though I had not yet met Uday, we had exchanged over a hundred emails. I had used bits of information from those emails to build a picture of him. I understood he would make a great father because he had worked with children. I judged that his heart was in the right place, and he had unusual courage, because he had served as a UN volunteer in the war-torn zones of Bosnia. His emails were well written, and our exchanges had been far from boring.

The way he had teased me about Dev, Zaid, and even Suraj, meant that there was nothing I would ever have to hide from him. He said he cooked very well. That bit, I figured later, was a plain white lie, but it meant that he didn't see the kitchen as a place only for women. Looking at the way he had lived his life, I could see that he too had followed his heart.

'There is nothing about this guy I do not like, and there is not a single reason why I should *not* marry him,' I tried to convince Shiv.

There was a long pause. He tried to understand what I was saying.

'And so you are moving to hell?' He finally broke into a smile, accepting my decision. 'Have you ever been to Chennai?

Don't tell me I didn't warn you. For a Bombay girl, Chennai is hell!'

Several years later I came across a book called *Blink* written by Malcolm Gladwell. The book lauds intuitive, spontaneous judgment. It says that our sixth sense is sharpened based on what we experience and, decisions made on these, even though they may appear to be guess work, are rather logical. Our mind, in time, allows us to see things based on highly developed skills that are supported with experience and knowledge.

So, a few years later, thanks to Malcolm Gladwell, I got the opportunity to understand that when I decided to marry Uday *Blink* had happened to me. My life had made me Wise Enough to be Foolish.

Chapter 47

Dev still didn't believe I was going to marry Uday. Though he had arrived on the scene before Uday, we had nothing between us. I had hoped that at an opportune moment I would tell him about Uday, but things had changed suddenly over dinner that night. Viren and I never saw each other again. Eventually, he married a sweet vegetarian south Indian girl his mother chose for him. My life got just too busy for us to stay in touch, but he is still a part of my US-vacation album.

Uday and I had decided to meet in December, yet he came to see me six days after I returned to India. That was the first time we met. He was so tall — six feet and six inches! I had never in my life known anyone that tall. As I stood on the chair to hug him, it felt like we had always known each other. And, within minutes of our first meeting, he asked me the question. It was preceded by a very short speech.

'I have never, in my entire life, met a woman worth fighting the last inch of the earth for, but you are that woman to me. Will you marry me?'

That, according to him, was his proposal to me. I could have accepted it without fuss, except that I had already proposed to a man in a two-word email — a man I had never met or spoken to, sitting exactly at the opposite end of the world, while I was in the United States of America on a vacation sponsored by my ex-husband.

'Too late, honey. I already beat you to it.'

We couldn't keep our hands off each other, and we didn't have to. He had every bit of passion that Arians are known for. He had come to see me for the weekend, and we did not leave my apartment even for a minute. It was only twenty days since we had first written to each other.

Uday was born a Hebbari Iyengar. That made my mother very happy. A Brahmin boy at last! I really must have done something right in my life to have the honour of going to a pure-bred family. And, in turn, my children could now have the same opportunity.

Although Uday lived in Chennai, he was actually from Bangalore. His house was less than a mile away from the school I had studied in eleven years ago. His aunt turned out to be Saiff's best friend at the time he had changed my life by asking me out on a date (that never happened). I was back exactly where I had started.

The following week I was on my way to meet his family and... I missed my flight!

Chapter 48

Uday's father had a striking resemblance to my father. His mother, on the other hand, was older and more traditional than my mother. But, below the surface of an ordinary south Indian family was an incredibly broad-minded set of people, starting with his eighty-one-year-old grandmother — the president of the White House (that is what they jokingly called their home), who belonged to an era when boys and girls were married to each other in their early teens, without meeting or even speaking to each other till the day they became man and wife.

But she was something else. After mothering four boys, she had learnt to play golf and drive her own car. She was the chattiest and bubbliest granny I had ever met. One afternoon as we sat talking on the porch of her house, to my amazement, she brought up the topic of live-in relationships. She didn't pass any judgment on the new generation abandoning the institution of marriage. Nor did she advocate marriage as the ultimate stamp of approval on a man-woman relationship. She accepted everything as a sign of the changing times.

Uday and his siblings had been brought up a bit differently. His brother had taken off to Israel to become a kibbutznik (a member of the Kibbutz traditional farming community), and returned to teach German before moving on to other things. Uday had gone to the UK to work with mentally challenged children after completing an MBA programme. His sister had married a man of her choice and moved to the US. They had chosen their spouses without the prejudice of religion, caste, creed, language, or even nationality. Uday had been married to an Englishwoman earlier, and he was not the first in the family to marry a foreigner. His parents were not offended, worried, or insecure about the children making different choices that appealed to them.

They had the freedom to question, and go against the tide — the freedom necessary to facilitate growth and change in a society.

Uday's father had lived in Germany for many years, and he loved his beer. Every evening he had a pint and, at times, his children joined him — the sons and the daughter. And the daughters-in-law.

I wondered if it would be disrespectful to drink in front of them as I had been brought up believing. And then I figured that respect did not come from drinking or not drinking in front of elders. It was reflected in how I behaved after I had downed that drink. This was the place where I could be anything I wanted to be. There were no expectations from me to please anyone, no judgments, just unconditional acceptance.

Chapter 49

I returned to Bombay for the last time. That New Year was not just the beginning of another year — it was the start of a new century, a new millennium and for me — a new life. And then, I celebrated my twenty-eighth birthday on January 4, 2000. It was my last birthday as a Bombay girl. In twenty-eight years I had had more drama in my life than most girls, and possibly more than some boys, would ever have in an entire lifetime. My house was overflowing with people who mattered to me, and who had come into my life for a reason.

Uday has been a huge hit with my friends. He is the sort of person who doesn't judge anyone or anything. He is quiet, strong, and self-assured, and is not threatened by anyone or anything, least of all my ambitions. I could be the next Bill Gates of the travel industry, or have my mug-shot on the front page of every newspaper but, to him, I am simply his girl. He doesn't get drawn into loud arguments, and getting angry with him is pointless because he pays no attention to anyone throwing a temper tantrum. He is a person who will drive me a hundred miles to see a friend, only because I don't know how to drive!

Time and again I ask myself: did I really just get lucky in my search for love? Was it just a coincidence that we met?

No one knows. From someone ungettable, to one who went to jail, to a Parsee priest, all the way to the one I will always love, to the man I eloped and married — it was a wild journey. And, finally, I had found love — in a man who was very like me in some ways. We both followed no religion, we both wanted children, and most of all, we both wanted a peaceful relationship.

But we are also very different. I have spent my younger years broke, and so, I am more of a capitalist, most of his friends are trying to change the world, so he is a socialist. I want to live the good life, he wants only as much as he needs. I love to dress up, and he's a 'minimalist'. I love big watches, he doesn't own a watch. My life has made me street-smart, his has made him trusting. I love to be a sportswoman, he loves to watch sports. I love big cities, he likes small villages. He likes to read, and I like to write. I love to travel, and he loves to come back home. He likes Pavarotti, and I love Elvis. My fiery, hot-blooded temper annoys his calm, level-headed Iyengari genes, and his quietude gets on my nerves. We are the perfectly imperfect couple.

And, as time goes by, I'm becoming a bit like him, and he is becoming like me. It is a crazy type of love. Yet it is like a candle — that gives warmth and lasts longer — like Rayo once described it.

Chapter 50

My parents were so relieved I was getting married again! 'Remarried' is so much a nicer tag than 'divorcee'. All these months they had not been able to tell anyone that my marriage was on the rocks. Now they could announce that not only had my marriage been on the rocks, I had even found myself another husband! And therefore a discussion about the divorce became immediately redundant. They had no reason to be embarrassed any more.

As far as I was concerned, they had failed the ultimate test of parenting. And, for them, I had failed their ultimate test as a child. Maybe if I had had the chance to see them every day, I would have had the opportunity to build the broken bridges, but the memories of the relationship were unhappy, and that was all I was left with. Over the years I built thick walls between them and myself. My resentment grew to a level where I could not spend a day with them without exchanging a few bitter words.

'There is not a relationship in your life you have not maintained. You love people, and people love you. Why is there so much animosity between you and our parents? If you can forgive Zaid, why can't you forgive them?' asked Nandini.

'I can get another man in my life, but not another set of parents.'

My parents had been my first heroes. The sadness of no acceptance from them would remain with me forever.

'Okay,' said Nandini, 'we are not going to spoil this day for you. But you do know you are the black sheep of the family — the blackest you can get. And I love you.'

Chapter 51

Uday and I were married in a temple, four hours' drive from Bangalore, where his grand-uncle and aunt got married two generations ago. My story started with a temple, and thus it seemed the most logical place to end and begin a new story. This temple was also the most magical place for a wedding. Built in the thirteenth century, this proposed UNESCO heritage site was a beautiful example of typical Hoysala sculpture. Uday's sister-in-law decorated the wedding altar with flowers and mango leaves. We had more than a hundred guests. I wore a sari he had chosen for me. We were married less than four months from the day he had first written to me.

As the priest muttered prayers binding us in holy matrimony, Uday said to me, 'I have a surprise for you.'

'A bullock-cart to take me home?' I laughed.

I did go home in a bullock cart and this is how our telepathy worked from the day we first wrote to each other.

And, even though I didn't know it when I asked him to marry me, it turned out that while Uday could not exactly buy me a holiday home in Monte Carlo, he had enough to take care of me if I ever chose not to work. But the jackpot I hit marrying Uday was not what he had in the bank. Uday had the largest happy family I had ever seen in my life. He had five uncles and aunts from his mother's side, and three from his father's side. He had over a dozen cousins of all ages, shapes, and sizes, and he was the eldest.

Now, they had all become my family. So, I was right when I had told Shiv: no risk, no gain.

His mother gave me a beautiful antique necklace. I wore a red sari she had bought me, when I set foot into the house as his wife. I bent forward and touched her feet, like many Indian daughters-in-law do. She hugged me, and, in a single line, gave me a blessing every mother should give her daughter: 'I want you only to be happy — always.'

This is all that was expected of me.

She was my Amma now — my mother. It had been a very long journey. Now I was home.

EPILOGUE

I moved to Chennai and got a job with another airline within a month. Shiv was right that Chennai was hell, especially for a fair-skinned Punjabi girl from Bombay who spoke no Tamil, and loved her butter chicken! We moved to Bangalore two years later when I started my own travel company (that still exists). And then, one evening in 2005, I had an unplanned dinner with two Americans who were visiting India. I invited them out as a courtesy any Indian would extend to visitors. I ended up with a dream job with the world's largest coach-touring company. I had not applied for the position, and they had not interviewed me for it. It only meant that I was still God's child and, as always, He knew best. And yes, the first time I was to go to the US to meet them, I missed my flight!

Subsequently, to combine my passion for active fun with my passion for travel, I founded The Active Holiday Company, India's first travel company focused only on adventure trips overseas.

In 2010, Uday and I celebrated our tenth wedding anniversary. I am ten kilos heavier, my hair is turning grey, and I can never make up my mind whether I should leave it as it is as a sign of wisdom or colour it. Even though he denies it, I see signs of wrinkles, but I am still the one woman in the world to him. We have two daughters, an even number. He disciplines them, while I teach them to break rules; he checks their homework, and I encourage them to dream.

Gayatri, with whom I had gone to Siddhi Vinayak Temple the night before I found out about Zaid and Maria's affair, died an unnatural death in 2001. My second daughter has been named after her. 'Gayatri' is a prayer for protection.

My elder daughter is called Aprajita. This was my name when I was born, until my parents changed it to Gauri a few months later. Aprajita means invincible.

I will always be a Bombay girl at heart. November 26, 2008, the day of the terrorist attacks on my city and my old office, was one of the saddest days of my life.

*My sister married her boyfriend whom I had visited in LA —
an Iyer boy from Chennai, and Uday gave her away. They have two
children.*

*My Math teacher set up his own classes. When I ran my first
half marathon more than twenty years after school, he sent me a
message on my phone, 'Good going, girl. Who were you chasing?'*

I replied: 'An ambition!'

*Nicky has a successful career. He married a girl who shared
her birthday with me. I always teased him that if he really wanted
to marry someone born on January 4, all he had to do was ask me
when I was fifteen!*

*Rayo eventually sold his company, and did all the things
he always wanted to do. He is very proud of my professional
accomplishments, and occasionally enjoys reminding me of our first
trip in Berlin, 'Your dressing sense has improved tremendously over
the years, darling.'*

*Rima lives in Bombay, and has a very successful career as an
architect. She is still single and very available. We had an incredible
reunion with Asha and Riya to celebrate our 20th year of meeting.*

*Suraj will always be the sun in my life. He eventually met a
beautiful girl and married her. They have two lovely children, and
he does not live with his parents.*

*Shiv runs a successful PR company, and broke up with his
bratty girlfriend. He is in a serious relationship with a Punjabi girl.
His father died a peaceful death.*

*Hiten and Jigna are still together. He still has extra-marital
relationships, and she never went to work. On the outside, they look
like a perfectly happy and beautiful couple.*

*After an exceptional career in the industry, Kamal set up her
own travel company with her husband. Her children are grown up,
and they are the best brought up kids I know.*

*My ex-sister-in-law still lives in New York. She has met my new
family, and I send her my kids' pictures every year.*

*My relationship with my mother remains estranged though we
try to keep it peaceful for the sake of my children who deserve and
love their grandparents. My father and I remained the imperfect
father and daughter till he passed away.*

Zaid married Maria in 2001. He has three children. I have stayed in touch with him. I asked him once if his life had been worth it.

'The honest answer is yes and no, but if I had to live my life all over again, I would make different choices,' he said.

And, although he did not ask me, I said, 'It's strange... I took a gamble and got exactly what I wanted from life.'

∽

I have been to Kruger National Park; I have seen the Great Wall of China; I have explored the Pyramids; I have trekked to the Base Camp of Mt. Everest to admire the majesty of the Himalayas; I have enjoyed many musicals. And though I discovered the Tuscan vineyards quite alone, I have shared a pitcher of wine with an incredibly cute Italian sitting by a lake in a little village in Europe. Someday in the future I will see Mt Fuji, climb the Kilimanjaro, snorkel in the Great Barrier Reef, and participate in the London Triathalon. I will host an art exhibition of my own paintings, run a very successful Active Holiday Company and who knows, one day I may even learn to drive!

JAICO PUBLISHING HOUSE
Elevate Your Life. Transform Your World.

ESTABLISHED IN 1946, Jaico Publishing House is home to world-transforming authors such as Sri Sri Paramahansa Yogananda, Osho, The Dalai Lama, Sri Sri Ravi Shankar, Robin Sharma, Deepak Chopra, Jack Canfield, Eknath Easwaran, Devdutt Pattanaik, Khushwant Singh, John Maxwell, Brian Tracy and Stephen Hawking.

Our late founder Mr. Jaman Shah first established Jaico as a book distribution company. Sensing that independence was around the corner, he aptly named his company Jaico ('Jai' means victory in Hindi). In order to service the significant demand for affordable books in a developing nation, Mr. Shah initiated Jaico's own publications. Jaico was India's first publisher of paperback books in the English language.

While self-help, religion and philosophy, mind/body/spirit, and business titles form the cornerstone of our non-fiction list, we publish an exciting range of travel, current affairs, biography, and popular science books as well. Our renewed focus on popular fiction is evident in our new titles by a host of fresh young talent from India and abroad. Jaico's recently established Translations Division translates selected English content into nine regional languages.

Jaico's Higher Education Division (HED) is recognized for its student-friendly textbooks in Business Management and Engineering which are in use countrywide.

In addition to being a publisher and distributor of its own titles, Jaico is a major national distributor of books of leading international and Indian publishers. With its headquarters in Mumbai, Jaico has branches and sales offices in Ahmedabad, Bangalore, Bhopal, Bhubaneswar, Chennai, Delhi, Hyderabad, Kolkata and Lucknow.

SINCE 1946